THE
SIX
WHO
CAME
TO
DINNER

stories

www.penguin.co.uk

Also by Anne Youngson

MEET ME AT THE MUSEUM
THREE WOMEN AND A BOAT

ANNE YOUNGSON

THE SIX WHO CAME TO DINNER

stories

doubleday

TRANSWORLD PUBLISHERS
Penguin Random House, One Embassy Gardens,
8 Viaduct Gardens, London SW11 7BW
www.penguin.co.uk

Transworld is part of the Penguin Random House group of companies
whose addresses can be found at global.penguinrandomhouse.com

Penguin
Random House
UK

First published in Great Britain in 2022 by Doubleday
an imprint of Transworld Publishers

'The Ballad of William Bloat' on pp. 129–130 by Raymond Calvert.
Illustrations by Matthew Hollings.

A CIP catalogue record for this book
is available from the British Library.

ISBN 9780857528254

Typeset in 11.25/15pt Adobe Garamond Pro by Jouve (UK), Milton Keynes
Printed and bound in Great Britain by Clays Ltd, Elcograf S.p.A.

The authorized representative in the EEA is Penguin Random House Ireland,
Morrison Chambers, 32 Nassau Street, Dublin D02 YH68.

Penguin Random House is committed to a sustainable
future for our business, our readers and our planet. This book
is made from Forest Stewardship Council® certified paper.

For Bev, Ceri, Elizabeth and Rebecca,
partners in story-telling

CONTENTS

THE SIX WHO
CAME TO DINNER

'I heard the bone snap,' said Theo.

'I knew at once,' said Vi. 'I knew it was serious.'

They turned towards each other as they spoke, tossing the storyline back and forth, relaxed in the way they sat, side by side, on a two-seater sofa upholstered in gold velvet. There were eight people in the room, all of us full of good food, all of us sitting comfortably, in the spacious, dimly lit, well-furnished lounge of our hostess, Miranda Peabody. I had never met Theo and Vi before but they appeared to be a successful, lately young couple, holding still to the illusion of youth. There was a chance I would know them better by the end of the evening, as it was set to be a long one.

Theo and Vi were in the middle of a story about their walking holiday in the Auvergne; more specifically, the occasion on their walking holiday in the Auvergne when Vi jumped off a wall and broke her ankle. It was a story, I could tell, that they had told many times before, as a couple. They were humorous in the parts that involved their own stupidity or discomfiture:

'Of course,' (Theo) 'my mobile had run out of charge and Vi's mobile was . . . remind me, darling?'

'On the bedside table at the hotel. Of course!' (Rueful smiles exchanged.)

They were sentimental in the parts that involved someone other than themselves.

'He just dropped the spanner he was holding – I mean, literally just let go of it, not waiting to put it down – and ran to the quad bike, shouting to his wife to call the doctor. His wife said: "I don't know any doctors because we are never ill, but I will find one."'

It was a nicely framed story. The brightness of the cold day, the starkly beautiful landscape, the view from the peak where the incident occurred. Just enough detail for us to be able to picture the scene, sympathize with or admire the participants, all the way through to the happy ending: arrival back in the UK with a perfectly set ankle and no more than a few weeks' worth of impaired mobility ahead. It was almost possible to overlook the consuming banality of the little tale. All six of us, in the audience, listened attentively to the end. This, though, had more to do with the instructions our hostess had given us at the start of the evening than with the quality of the story and its telling.

'I can't bear it when people take it in turns to talk about something that has happened to them,' she said, over the pre-dinner drinks. 'For one thing, no one listens because they are busy working out what similar story of their own experience they can start to tell when whoever is talking shuts up. And for another, some people grab more turns in the speaker's chair and others never get to share their own, just as interesting anecdote.'

There was general agreement. Theo told us the story of a party he had been to where the host spent the entire evening explaining how he had built the house, starting with the purchase of the land and progressing through design, planning permission, foundations, up to and including the fitting of the loo seat and the fixing of the knocker on the front door. Our hostess waited for him to finish then made a proposal, or, rather, dictated a plan for how she wanted the evening to run. Each of us, she said, could tell one story. It could be any story from the distant or recent past and could be as long or as short as we chose to make it. Whatever story anyone else told, we could – indeed should – discuss and comment on.

But we could not use it as a springboard for another. Or, if we did, that was our only turn, gone.

'We'll start after dinner,' she said. 'That will give you all time to plan in your mind what you're going to say and leave you free to concentrate on those who go before you.'

As well as Theo and Vi, there was one other couple among the eight of us, Carl and Maeve. They could tell one story each, Miranda said to the couples, or one together.

Now I realize I have set off relating the events of that evening from the point when things began to be interesting: that is, from the first story told. When really I should have begun with the other guests or, more properly, with the hostess. She was a woman in her sixties, familiar to me as a neighbour, but not one of my familiars; someone I had known for some while as a member of the society I mixed with in the village, but she was a private person and, in truth, I knew almost nothing about her. I still don't, but I do know her to be even more formidable than I had thought her before this dinner party. Of the other people in the room, I knew two of them at least as well as I knew Miranda, had a passing acquaintance with another two, and had never met Theo and Vi before.

The two I thought I knew quite well were Solomon Thorogood and Berenice, whose surname, being Polish, I have never learned to spell or even pronounce; she is always addressed as Mrs B by the people who don't feel they want to attempt her full name. Solomon is a retired solicitor, a dry man who spends his life indoors and is an expert on Venetian glass. A widower, so I understand. Berenice is also a widow, or at least lives alone; she is very well dressed and fading into old age in an elegant way, retaining a restful beauty. What she says is in keeping with her appearance, sounding well put and meaningful. They are both perfect dinner party guests, if not very interesting ones. By the end of the evening, I would be able to make a much better judgement on both.

The couple I knew only slightly were unlike the rest of us in the room. Carl Turner and Maeve. I don't know Maeve's other name. It might even be Turner. Carl is a gardener and therefore known to almost everyone in this village, where the people who can afford to have other people labour on their behalf greatly outnumber those prepared to so labour. It is a large village; what Carl has to offer is hard to find, and his time is fiercely contested. Maeve is a care assistant at the local nursing home, a converted manor set in its own park. She has a particularly engaging face; round, freckled, wide mouth, fringe of red curls. I have always liked women who look like Maeve. I married one, once. Where is she now, I wonder? Carl is big and solid and has fingers thickened to sausages through years of manual labour in the wet and the cold. Though not so many years, in fact. Both he and Maeve are younger than the rest of us; a decade younger than Theo and Vi, I imagine. Two decades younger than I am.

Strangely enough – and this must be a credit to Miranda Peabody's skills as a hostess – it did not occur to me until towards the end of Theo and Vi's broken-ankle story what a strange collection of guests this was. How odd, that Miranda should have invited two comfortably off, withered old people, a thrusting mid-life career couple, two young people in jobs regarded as low skilled (because the skills they had were useful rather than exploitable for large gains) and me. How shall I describe myself? Middle-aged, middle class, middle income? So I present myself; and the first of these at least is true. My name is Henry.

The funny-but-of-course-essentially-serious story of the trip to France drew to a close. The rest of us, who had been entirely silent throughout, followed Miranda's lead in implying interest and attention when it ended.

'I've always found the French to be helpful and friendly,' she said.

'I've never been to France,' said Berenice, 'but I would love to go.'

'I expect you were wearing the wrong sort of shoes,' said Solomon.

'I don't know what would happen to us if Carl broke his leg,' said Maeve, and he took her hand and shook his head at her as if denying such a possibility existed.

'That was a good start,' I said. 'I'm looking forward to the other stories.'

'I'll go next,' said Solomon. 'As a contrast.'

The story he told was indeed a contrast. No action, no detail, no weather or landscape. Instead, he chose a dilemma he had been faced with in the years when he was still working. Some years ago, he had been involved in a case of alleged child abuse, acting on behalf of the accused. Two couples – one without children, one with a daughter of eight years old or so – had become close friends. They lived near each other, went on holiday together, the one babysat for the other, they fed each other's cats and watered each other's tomato plants and wandered in and out of each other's houses at will. Until the mother of the young girl accused the husband of the childless woman of abusing her child. The case never went to trial. The accused man was vehement in his denial, supported by his wife. They could only imagine, they said, that the allegations had been prompted by some jealousy on the part of the parents, who had less freedom to enjoy themselves and less money to do it with. Solomon's client said, in private, that he was afraid the accusing wife was secretly in love with him and had chosen this way of making him notice her. It was possible, his wife said, sadly, that the father of the child might in fact be the abuser and the mother was in denial and seeking someone else to blame.

At length, the authorities concluded that there was

insufficient evidence, and convinced the mother and father to let it go, to avoid putting their child through the ordeal of a trial. When the police, in Solomon's presence, reported this outcome to the accused, they also told him that they had taken note of him; that they would know him again if anything similar occurred in the future. Solomon felt the same. He could not like the man and for all he wished to believe him, he did not. It was a relief to him (and significant, he could not help but feel) that it was the accused couple who moved away, and he heard no more of them.

Some time later, a divorcee with a young daughter, for whom he had acted in the divorce and in the subsequent selling of one house and buying of another, came in to consult him. She was in a relationship, she told him, and her partner was about to move in with her. Marriage was possible. She wanted to know what his advice was in relation to the making of a new will, the ownership of the house. This was a woman he liked. He applauded her good sense in seeking such advice and they talked through the possible advantages and disadvantages of letting the new man in her life be a partner in all her financial affairs. Speaking hypothetically, Solomon laid out the problems that could arise if the man turned out to be unreliable, untrustworthy, fickle. He did not think it likely his client would have chosen unwisely. Until, almost on parting, she mentioned the name of the man who had been the subject of their conversation. It was the husband accused, some years before, of the abuse of a child of a similar age to his client's daughter. What, he asked, should he have done?

This story was interrupted frequently with requests for clarification, but, with a few detours back over territory already covered, the tale was told and the question understood. There were two or three lamps lit in the drawing room where we sat, and the polished wood and heavy fabrics of the furnishings were so many pools of darkness around the edge. The expressions on the guests' faces were hard to identify, unless they leaned into the light or showed extreme emotion. I looked at Miranda, waiting for her to speak first, and I sensed the others, too, were waiting for her lead, but I could not tell from her face what she thought.

'An interesting dilemma,' she said, finally. 'Professional and compassionate obligations would compel you to say nothing. But if harm came to the mother and her child as a result, you would have made yourself complicit.'

'I think you should have told her,' said Berenice. 'Poor woman, all alone. You can't imagine how hard it is, to be a woman, living alone.'

'Hang on,' said Theo. 'This is someone who has never been found guilty of anything. What would you say? He was once accused of something he probably didn't do? What a way to destroy someone's life.'

'Two people's lives,' Vi said. 'Even if she didn't believe

it, the woman would never feel as safe and happy with the man again.'

'I would say it was none of your business,' I said. 'Who are you to make judgements?'

'You could have kept an eye on her,' said Carl. 'You know, watched out for her, not spying as such, just noticing, if you know what I mean.'

Miranda leaned forward into the light and the expression on her face was puzzling: pleased, but suspicious.

'Well done,' she said to Carl, 'well done.'

'I'll go next,' said Berenice.

'Hold on a minute,' said Miranda. 'What did you do, Solomon? We need this story to have an ending, as well as a beginning and a middle.'

'I said nothing, of course,' said Solomon, smoothing the material of his mustard-coloured cord trousers over his knees as if checking they had been correctly made, with the nap going downwards. 'I'm not quite sure how my young friend here thinks I could have, as he put it, "kept an eye on her", but obviously I made sure she knew she could consult me about anything in the future.'

'Did she?' asked Vi.

'No, actually. Really, I don't know what you're all expecting. This isn't a story in a book where the ends are neatly tied up. This is life. It was the dilemma that inter-ested me; the ethical question. If you must know, the couple moved away, so I have no idea whether they lived happily ever after or if it ended in tragedy.'

'What were the names?' asked Theo, getting his phone out. 'I could google them and find out if they've featured in the news.'

'I think Solomon would prefer us not to know,' said Miranda. 'Over to you, Berenice.'

Berenice's story was short and yet full of irrelevant detail, most of which I will eliminate. One evening, she said, when it was nearly dark, the wind blowing strongly in the conifers round her isolated cottage, far from the nearest street lamp, there was a knock at the door. She opened it, as far as the chain would allow, and peered through the gap. A man stood outside, unknown to her, dressed in jeans and a waterproof jacket with a knitted beanie on his head and a dog on the end of a lead.

'I'm sorry to bother you,' he said, 'but there is a cat in your gateway and it seems to have been injured in some way.'

He stood back and moved his arm to indicate the gate, lost in the darkness behind him.

'A cat,' said Berenice.

'Yes. I'll show you.'

Here Berenice's story moved from the what to the why, from action to analysis; that is, the man's possible motives for wanting to lure her, a lone, defenceless woman, out of the house. Stepping across the threshold would have put her in his power. Any attack hidden by darkness, any cries inaudible above the wind, even if – and this was unlikely – anyone was close enough to have heard them. What, she speculated, was he doing, out after dark; was the dog a prop to give him a feasible motive for being there or part of the plot, ready to hold her at bay while he ransacked the house?

'I thought you said it was a Labrador,' Maeve said. 'I've never known a vicious Labrador.'

Berenice looked from Maeve, who is quite a solid young person, to Carl, who is positively well built, and nodded, investing the nod and the direction of her gaze with meaning.

'Ah, but you've never been in my position,' she said, 'alone, and vulnerable,' dropping her voice on the last word.

Maeve looked puzzled, as well she might, but Berenice was back on her doorstep, enjoying herself. She was an animal lover, she said, and would be prepared to risk limb or indeed life if the situation arose where either of these could be effectively sacrificed for the removal of pain from one of God's little creatures. But in this case, she was quite clear that God would not have expected her to offer herself up for a possibly mythical cat which might or might not be injured. So she said to the man with the Labrador and the knitted hat:

'I don't have a cat,' and shut the door.

There was a pause during which Berenice looked

smug and no one spoke. It was not clear whether the story was over or, if so, what had made it worth telling. It turned out it was not over and the pause was for dramatic effect.

'The next morning,' said Berenice, 'I went down to the gate, and what do you think I found?' No one offered to speculate, so she told us, with a note of triumph in her voice. 'A dead cat!'

It crossed my mind to say the story was a dead end, but it was not a flippant gathering, so I kept quiet. No one else could think of anything to say, either, or nothing they wished to say out loud, except for Maeve who murmured: 'What a shame!' which was ambiguous enough to suit all of us.

'Thank you, Berenice,' said Miranda. 'Now, Henry' – turning to me – 'would you mind topping up everyone's glass, then I think we might have your story.'

I have a few stories I tell, carefully selected, edited and embellished, for just this sort of occasion. It means I can join in a conversation when I feel it is appropriate without finding I am revealing too much about myself by carelessly launching into an anecdote I have not reflected upon and thought through. I selected one of the humorous stories, as the dark night, the menacing figure at the door and the dead cat had left a gloomy taste on the palate. So I set off through a little tale involving a lift in an apartment block in Rio de Janeiro stuck for four hours between two floors. I described the people with me in the lift: the grandmother and her granddaughter who had been shopping for a party and took up, with their bags and boxes and not insubstantial bodies, the space of four people. The British boy on a gap year, wearing flip-flops and showcasing a bad attack of fungal nail infection on his right big toe. The American evangelist who was wearing too many clothes and whose bald head had started to drip even before the lift stopped moving. The two workmen who had been going up to paint the penthouse, one of them with a speech impediment, who had entered last, just squeezing themselves and their pots and tool-bags into the space available. And me. I described the way the conversation started, quite hesitantly and in at least two languages, then became general, ultimately jovial as the grandmother and the teenage girl concluded that the party might as well start early, and the bottles of red wine and the salty snacks were circulated. By the time the lift moved and the doors opened, the younger of the two painters and the granddaughter were writing each other's phone numbers on each other's bare arms; the grandmother was teaching the American the Portuguese word for everything within her eye-line, which, as she was now sitting on the floor, consisted mainly of parts of the body; the gap year student and I were seeing how many opening chess gambits we could remember and articulate clearly; and the painter with the speech impediment had nearly completed a painting of a mermaid on the inside of the door. The last of the bottles of red wine was empty and the authority figures gathered in the lobby, pressing forward to see if we had sustained any injury, were pushed aside by a group of people conscious only of their bladders, and were left contemplating a craggy landscape of empty snack packets.

At the end of this story, which had bemused Berenice ('But what were they going to give the guests at the party?') and irritated Solomon ('I don't know why anyone would waste their time travelling to places where you might know the lifts won't work') but amused the others, Miranda said:

'I wonder how much of that is actually true, Henry, dear.'

'Enough,' I said, having too much respect for Miranda to pretend it had all happened just as I described it.

Carl and Maeve had a story each. Before they began there was a flurry of movement, further topping up of glasses, trips to the loo. Theo and Vi, I noticed, were showing a tendency to have conversations with each other at a level just above a whisper but below audible. I was interested to see if, having had their ten minutes in the spotlight so early in the evening, they attempted to leave before the rest of the group had had their turn. Miranda must have made the same observations, and took Vi off into the kitchen on some pretext. When they came back, Vi murmured something to Theo and they settled back down as if the idea of abandoning the party had never crossed their minds.

Maeve went first and was brief.

'I don't really have a story,' she said. 'Nothing interesting or exciting has ever happened to me. At least' – she looked sideways at Carl – 'nothing I'd want to talk about in this company.'

Her eyes were beautiful, hazel, oval and thickly lashed.

'Nothing that didn't involve alcohol,' Carl said.

All of us except Solomon and Berenice smiled politely.

'So I'm going to tell you about something that really pleased me, in the home where I work,' said Maeve.

'Something that pleased you is perfect,' said Miranda. 'And it will be a story, I'm sure.'

'Well, it is, in a way.'

She told us about a woman with dementia who had moved into the home, because her husband could no longer manage. At first, she was unhappy and restless. She would not participate in any of the activities organized by the home for the residents; in fact, she did her best to disrupt them, throwing pieces of jigsaw on the floor, attempting to puncture the giant inflatable skittles, tearing up the pictures laid out to be the basis of memory boxes. Her husband, who visited every day, was told all this by the staff and he said, quietly, for he was a quiet man:

'She wants to be useful.'

The next day he brought in a laundry basket full of

socks. Individual socks, in different colours and patterns. Putting his hand on his wife's arm, he said: 'Help us with these,' and she did. For the first time she sat quietly for more than an hour, carefully selecting a sock, searching through the basket for another sock to match it, putting them together. When she had finished, her husband kissed her.

'Thank you,' he said.

The next morning, while the other residents sat in a circle singing or trying to sing or pretending to sing or just sitting while others sang, Maeve emptied the cutlery out of the drawer and muddled it up.

'Can you help me with this?' she said to the woman who had sorted the socks. 'I seem to be in a mess.'

The woman put the forks, the knives and the spoons back, in order, in the drawer. The husband brought something in every day for his wife to help him with – putting the right lids with the right empty jars, putting the photographs of their children growing up in the right order, sorting out the seed packets. Whenever she became angry, the staff found something for her to do that they could claim was helping them: tidying a cupboard, separating the pieces of two different jigsaws.

Maeve became slightly pink as she spoke. I could see it was not going to be easy for her to bring this little tale to a close. There could be no happy-ever-after for the man and his wife, yet most of her audience was watching her, maybe more fixedly than she had expected, as if hoping for something to come out of it that was more than a moment or two of peace for a damaged brain. She had not understood, I think, that her story would not be heard from her point of view, from the perspective of a carer admiring the ingenuity of the husband and the compassion of the staff. Though Theo and Vi may have seen it as she did, the rest of us were closer in age to the old woman and her husband than to Maeve, and we could not help but project ourselves forward into this ghastly future where sorting socks was the greatest pleasure we could expect from life.

'I think it shows,' said Maeve, reaching for a climax, 'that we have to remember the person that the person with dementia still is, when we try and help them.'

It was a good call. All of us could agree wholeheartedly with it, and relax.

Carl was equally brisk with a case of mistaken identity. One of his employers had a garden full, for reasons Carl could never understand, of mislabelled plants. A lilac with purple flowers was labelled 'Madame Lemoine', when Madame Lemoine has white flowers, and a clematis labelled '*viticella* Polish Spirit', a late-flowering cultivar, bloomed early and had pale-mauve bells in place of the flat, dark-purple heads the name would lead anyone in the know to expect. The garden's owner was proud of his plants and had become committed to the names he believed belonged to them. He reacted badly when Carl took out his phone and offered to call up evidence that this was not that lilac, not that clematis. So, in the interests of harmony, Carl agreed to accept the employer's word and remembered, most of the time, to use the right wrong name when referring to them. All was well until the garden owner took a notion to enter a specimen rose into the local flower show. He selected a stem from a bush he knew, with complete certainty, was Whisky Mac. Whisky Mac, Carl knew, and was pretty certain the judges and many of those attending the show would know, was apricot. The rose his employer picked and entered was deep crimson. It was also magnificent and duly won first prize, which resulted in a number of people asking the proud exhibitor if he knew what the rose was called. The next time Carl turned up for work he found his employer looking serious.

'Now, Carl,' he said. 'I'm disappointed in you. You told me that rose was called Whisky Mac, and now I find you were completely wrong. I was very embarrassed at the Flower Show, I have to tell you. Did you not realize that Whisky Mac is apricot?'

This story provoked quite a response. Theo wanted to know how these mistakes could possibly have occurred. The correct naming of things (speaking as an academic) was absolutely vital and he could not imagine what carelessness had crept into the horticultural world. Berenice said she could not see the point of the story. What did it matter? Miranda marvelled at the arrogance of the employer, believing it is always someone else who is wrong.

Carl looked pleased with the interest shown, though I suspect he had anticipated we would find it funny, as he clearly did, that anyone could be ignorant of such basic facts as the colour of a named rose or the flowering season of a named clematis.

Miranda took Maeve and Vi with her into the kitchen and came back with tea and coffee, plates of little buns, slices of cake, marzipan fruits and bowls of chocolates. It struck me how well choreographed this evening was turning out to be – the alcohol circulating just when it felt like the right time for another drink; tea and coffee appearing when the thought of something warm was just then forming; nuts and olives giving way to the rich little dainties. As these were handed round by Maeve (and what a pleasure it was to have the smooth arm, red curls and freckled face brought so close to my arm, and my face), Miranda turned up some of the lights so that the room stepped from cosy winter semi-darkness into brightness.

'That's nice,' said Berenice, pulling the cushion behind her into a more comfortable position and placing a slice of cake on the saucer of her teacup. I agreed with her; it was nice. I felt settled, even though I am habitually uneasy with careful choreographing (unless I have done it myself, of course) and even though I realized Miranda had encouraged us to expose ourselves in the stories we had been telling. Including me. For all my care, the one I had chosen told anyone listening that I was a man who liked to hang back and observe; someone detached. Solomon and Berenice had both shown us their obsession with self – Solomon needing to believe he was always right; Berenice needing to think of her own safety above anything else. Theo and Vi, from the story they had told, felt to me to have an emptiness at the core of their lives that needed to be filled by turning whatever they did into a story. Unlike Maeve, who possibly cared too much, Theo and Vi, I thought, probably had little emotion to spare for others. Carl, like Maeve, had limited horizons, but was committed to and proud of the field he understood.

Only Miranda was as much a mystery as she had been at the beginning of the evening.

'Are you going to tell us a story now?' asked Vi.

'Indeed I am,' said Miranda.

Now the lights had been turned up, we could see each other clearly as Miranda began to talk – each other and Miranda herself, her strong features, her severe haircut, her long, narrow fingers and long, narrow feet. She wore black linen trousers and a square-cut, dark-purple linen shirt, but these were not what held the eye.

'I am going to tell you a story,' she said, 'about a young man and what happened to him five years ago. His name, as it happens, was Robin, but that is not relevant to the story; you did not know him, and the story would have unrolled just the same whatever his name was. You do not need to know it to follow the story I am going to tell. Just as you do not need to know about his love of cheese, his dislike of having his hair washed, his inability to swim, his skill in untangling knotted string. What you do need to know is that he was twenty-two years old and he was ill with hepatitis C. He had been in hospital in London, having tests which confirmed the diagnosis, and had discharged himself against the doctors' advice because he did not feel safe in hospital. Nor, for reasons again outside the scope of this story, did he feel safe at the place he was living in at the time, so he set off for somewhere he would feel safe, which was a house here, in this village.

'He went from the hospital to Paddington Station and caught a train. It was this time of year, late October, and the forecasters had been warning of extreme weather conditions for some days before this, and, with increasing accuracy, of the amount of rain and the wind speeds that could be expected during the evening and overnight on this day, the day Robin left London. He had not heard any of the warnings and it would probably have made no difference to the decisions he made if he had done.

'The train was delayed again and again along the route and finally stopped, in a place a few miles from here, where there was once a station. The station was closed and the buildings converted into a house, but where the train stopped there were still the remains of a platform. The train manager walked through the carriage, saying they had information a tree had come down and was blocking the track just ahead of them. They had called for a maintenance crew to clear the line but so far they had no promises for when this might arrive. Some of the other passengers in the carriage with Robin declared themselves ready to go out and manhandle the tree off the track, if it was physically possible to do that, and the train manager said that wouldn't be allowed. Robin looked out of the window and saw another member of the train staff down on the remains of the platform, which made him think that somewhere on the train the doors were unlocked. He knew he was not far from his destination and he thought, if he could get out of here, he would be able to find a way of getting to the village without waiting for the train to move. Remember, he had not heard the weather forecast; he was ill and a little disorientated. Even before this happened, he had had no plan for how he was going to reach the place he was aiming for from the station where he had planned to leave the train. He had no mobile phone and no money. He was not expected at his destination. It seemed obvious, to him, that it was easier just to walk from this place, so he went along the train until he found the unlocked door, then jumped out.

'The wind was a surprise to him, and caught him off balance. He stumbled to the edge of the platform and sank to his knees, trying to get his breath. When he had recovered, he looked around and saw this was an isolated place. It was nearly, but not quite, dark and the only lights he could see were those in the converted station building. He turned back towards the train, thinking, after all, it might be safer to stay on it, but at that moment it started to move, the driver having climbed back on board while Robin was hunched on the grass. He had no alternative now. He made his way towards the lights.'

Miranda's voice was slow and deliberate. She spoke as if she expected her audience to pay attention. The rest of us had inserted asides and giggles as we spoke, stumbled over words, repeated ourselves, looked round to make sure our audience was still with us. Miranda did none of these things. And the audience was definitely with her. All of us almost literally on the edge of our seats. As Miranda let a pause develop, Vi said: 'That's where we live,' and Miranda nodded before carrying on with the story.

'Robin found he could hardly stand up, once the train had left and there was no shelter from the wind. Remember, he was ill. He had thought he would walk past the lit house, if he could be sure of the direction he was going, or maybe knock and check on which way was west, but by the time he reached the door he thought he might not have the strength to go further, so he lifted the knocker and let it fall then sat down on the step, arms over his head to protect himself from the force of the gale.'

'I remember that night,' said Theo. 'Who wouldn't? It was epic. I don't think we would have heard the door if someone had knocked, would we, darling?'

'I think we did hear something,' said Vi.

'Lots of things!' said Theo, and laughed, then smoothed his face at once. 'I mean, there were bits of tree flying about and the shed roof was completely gone in the morning.'

'We must have missed his knock,' said Vi, who did not look like laughing, 'in the turmoil.'

'Weren't you looking out of the window to see if there was any damage?' said Solomon.

'It was dark,' said Theo, 'and at the best of times it wouldn't have been easy to see if there was anyone outside, but as well' – he shrugged – 'in those conditions, it wouldn't have been possible to tell if it was a man waving his arms or a bush thrashing about in the wind.'

Miranda continued as if no one had spoken.

'When there was no answer, Robin walked round the house, looking through the lighted windows, but although he thought the people inside had seen him, they made no move to let him in. There was a signpost a little further down the road and he went that way, knowing he could check his direction when he reached it. He found he was walking towards the village, although the signpost also told him he was six miles away from it. But what option did he have? He kept walking.

'After the signpost he came to a stretch of lane with cottages on each side. Only a couple of these had lights in the windows, but the buildings were shielding Robin from the worst of the wind so he thought, maybe, he could walk the six miles, arrive at the house where he knew he would feel safe without having to ask for help from strangers. So he did not knock on any of the doors. Beyond the cottages the woods grew thickly up to the verge and Robin felt his decision was the right one. He was a young man, after all. The walk was not so long. He managed a mile before the woods were replaced by open fields and the first gust that caught him, unexpectedly, knocked him sideways into a barbed-wire fence which tore the flesh on the hand he put out to save himself and ripped the sleeve of the jacket he wore, already too slight a garment for the conditions, now almost worse than useless as the wind kept catching the material where it had been ripped and using it as a lever to push and pull at Robin's frail body.

'He kept going. What else could he do? Every time he passed a tree or a stretch of hedge that provided a moment of relative shelter, he paused, catching his breath. At one such pause, a branch broke off the tree he was sheltering beside and tore his ear on the way down, bruising his shoulder. After that, he only stopped where there was a gate or a piece of strong fencing he could lean against, turned with his back to the wind, while he built up enough resolution to continue his journey. At last, after another mile or so, he saw a light in a building some little way off the road. He couldn't see what sort of building it was as there were trees round it, hiding it from view, but he was sure the light was shining from a window, and this must be a place where one or more people were collected, in the shelter and warmth.

'As he turned off the road down the driveway, the wind, as it is in the nature of winds to do, dropped suddenly. Up until then there had been gusts of abnormal ferocity, but in between these, it had still been a gale, with no respite, no moment when the hat on your head (only Robin was wearing no hat) would not have been ripped off if not securely fastened. It was still blowing hard, just not as hard, and as Robin passed into the trees round the house, it felt calm. Maybe, he thought, if whoever was inside would come to the door and let him in to rest a moment, have a drink of water, he would be able to go the rest of the way.'

I did not want this story to continue. But Miranda was not looking at me, and no one was going to stop her now.

'It was a small cottage, but the windows facing the road on the ground floor were lit up, the curtains not yet drawn, and Robin saw a movement behind the glass.

There was a bell and a knocker on this door, and he used them both. This time he would not leave without asking for help.'

'I was living in that cottage,' I said. 'Five years ago. I was having work done on my house and it was easier to move out and rent. It was a holiday let, in the summer, so available all winter.'

Miranda looked at me and nodded. I don't know if she was acknowledging that she knew this, or accepting what I said.

'So it was you who lent him a bike,' she said.

There was a brief diversion as Solomon kicked over a cup he had set down on the floor beside his chair, and the dribble of coffee had to be mopped up, the cup cleared away.

I remembered that night. I remembered the young man at the door. I had taken him for a vagrant, wandering about in the dark, off his head on drugs or drink, with his unsteady stance, torn clothing and blood-streaked face. Had I been alone I might have taken him in and tried to establish who I could call to come and collect him. But I was not alone and I did not want it known who was with me, so the boy was a most unwelcome intrusion. If the lights had stayed on, it would have made no difference to the way I treated him but, luckily, they went out, and that made it easier to justify my actions to Miranda. To avoid, let me be frank, telling the whole truth.

'Shall I explain what happened next,' I said, when the crisis with Solomon's cup had been resolved.

'If you like,' said Miranda.

'I had friends staying with me, and we were talking and laughing and what with that and the almost unbearable noise of the wind thrashing about in the conifers round the property and the rattling of the windows, I might not have heard the knock or the ring. But, as Miranda has said, the wind dropped at that moment and, as it happened, I was in the hallway at the time, on my way to the kitchen, so I heard both and opened the door.

'It was impossible to see clearly who was on the doorstep. It was a dark night and the cottage had no outside light, or not one that worked. I could guess this was someone young, and male, but otherwise, hand on heart, I could tell nothing about him except I didn't know him. I didn't notice his clothing was torn, or unsuitable for the conditions, or that he was ill. I know that now and of course it would have made a difference, if I'd been able to take that in at the time.

'He had just begun to explain he was trying to reach the village, when all the lights went out. A tree had fallen on a substation somewhere miles away and the whole district lost supply for more than twelve hours, as I'm sure we all remember. I had been on the point of inviting him in out of the weather, and had the lights stayed on I would have done. Then, of course, I would have seen the state he was in and would have driven him to the village myself. As it was, I was caught between wanting to help this stranger and being anxious to get back to my friends, who were left in the dark, and already calling out to me to ask for candles and torches.

'As I took him for a fit young man, and the wind had dropped, and the village was only two or three miles away, I told him he could take the bicycle that was round the corner of the house, leaning against the wall. It belonged to the cottage and I hadn't used it, but it had looked to me to be in working order, if not exactly shiny and new. I thought it possible I might never see it again – forgive me for saying that young men who knock on the doors of isolated properties after dark do not necessarily inspire confidence – but I could replace it easily enough, and it seemed a good way of providing assistance to a stranger and also getting back to my friends, who I could hear crashing into things in the room where I had left them. The bike was gone in the morning, so I assumed it had been the answer. I never did see it again.'

I would have liked more time to construct this story, but I felt I had done well in pitching it as I had. I had no idea, though, what Miranda had been told about what actually happened, and though I had stuck to the facts – knock at door, man on doorstep, lights out, offer of bicycle – the actual interchange between myself and Robin, as I now knew he was called, was not precisely as I had described it. Miranda's face showed no awareness of anything amiss in the story I had told. But nor did it show recognition of a set of truths she already knew.

She took up the tale again.

'The bike Robin had been lent had no lights and in the darkness it was often difficult to tell where the edges of the road lay. And the wind became once more violent, blowing not into his face, which would have made it impossible to make progress, but from the side, which made it difficult to keep his balance. He had managed only half a mile or so when he heard a car coming up behind him. He knew that, in his dark clothing on a bike without lights, he would be close to invisible, so he stopped and stood on the verge, holding the bike. The car was travelling slowly and hugging the left-hand edge of the road as if the driver was nervous of straying off it. His headlights should have picked out Robin and the bike in plenty of time for the driver to alter his course to the small degree necessary to avoid them, moving the left-hand wheels away from the gutter on the road's edge a foot or two to the right. By the time Robin realized the driver was not going to react, it was too late. He lifted the bike at the last minute, hoping to pull it out of the path of the car, but the wing caught the bike's handlebars and pitched it, and Robin, tangled up with it, into the ditch.'

Miranda paused, catching no one's eye. No one spoke.

'The car was a vintage Jaguar,' she went on. 'An XK, I believe.'

'Good heavens!' said Solomon, sounding like an amateur actor with four lines to speak, failing to make those lines sound natural or spontaneous. 'That sounds like my car!'

'Could it have been?' asked Theo. 'I mean, were you about on that night? You must remember.'

'Yes, yes, I was,' said Solomon. 'I'd been to dinner with some old friends in town and I remember driving slowly because of the awful conditions – slower than normal, that is, because I am not a fast driver. I can never see the point of speeding up to take a matter of minutes off the arrival time. But I can't believe I would have struck a cyclist and not noticed.'

'Nevertheless, someone driving a vintage Jaguar, slowly, did do so,' said Miranda. 'And must have been aware of the impact.'

Solomon's face was mottled white and puce.

'Well, if your informant is reliable,' he said, 'I can only assume I thought I'd struck a tree branch fallen into the road. How dreadful.' He sat shaking his head, smoothing his trousers, and the rest of us sat watching him. 'I mean, if I'd known, I could have helped him. Out of the ditch and in any other way necessary.'

'Indeed,' said Miranda. 'As it was, Robin stayed in the ditch for a couple of hours. He was so exhausted it even felt like a relief, to be forced to lie down, to be able to stop pushing himself to reach the place he was travelling towards. The bike had landed on top of him and after he had made the effort to shift it, and had contemplated the new stings and aches from the new cuts and bruises, he fell into a sort of doze. He was roused by the tickling of some insect that had crawled into the tear in his trousers made by something sharp on the bike as it fell. He became aware of rustling which might or might not have been the wind; it was still dark. Slowly and painfully, becoming tangled once again in the bicycle, Robin climbed out of the ditch. He began to walk. It began to rain. This, too, had been forecast and was as heavy as the Met Office had warned it would be, only Robin had not heard them. The water reached inside his inadequate, ruined clothing and soaked his skin. He began to shiver.

'He was walking alongside a wall which, by its orderly nature, he took to be a garden wall. Where there was a garden there was likely to be a house, and even if the occupants of the previous two houses he had called at had rebuffed him, Robin was ready to try again. If the house proved inhospitable, he thought, then a garden would still be better, more comforting, than the wild trees and ditches. He looked for a gate; he found a gate and, though it was locked, it was possible for someone even in Robin's condition, and certainly for someone in a state of utter desperation, to climb over.

'On the other side of the wall, an expanse of lawn and shrubs stretched away into the darkness. There might or might not have been a house; there were deeper dark shapes in the darkness but no lights. This might have meant no house, or an empty house, or have been the result of the power cut. Near at hand, though, Robin could see a structure. A sort of summer house. Shelter, with a door that was not locked. Inside was a pile of wooden tables and chairs, folded up, one bench and a heap of cushions. Robin put some of the cushions on the bench and pulled the rest on top of him. He felt, for a moment, comfortable. He fell asleep.'

Carl had been leaning further and further forward in his chair. Maeve had taken his hand and was holding on to it as if she was tugging against his impulse to jump into the story too early.

'I found him,' Carl said. 'I found him.'

'I thought it was you,' said Miranda.

'Oh!' Carl released his hand from Maeve's and rubbed his face. 'I didn't realize he was ill. What I mean to say is, I thought he might be but I couldn't be sure if he was just drunk, you know, or on drugs? It wasn't even light; I could barely see him. I knew he needed help, that's for sure, but it wasn't a good morning, if you know what I mean. I'd been woken up by the police banging on my door, asking me to go and clear a tree that had come down blocking a road, and I'd left my chain oil in the summer house at this garden I look after, out of the village, so I suppose you could say all that was lucky because otherwise I wouldn't have been there. It wasn't my day for that garden. But the problem was, I had to get to this tree, and my mobile was flat – no power, you see, overnight – so I couldn't hang about and talk to this chap – well, to Robin, I should say – and I couldn't call anyone to come and help him.'

'So what did you do?' asked Solomon. 'Leave him there?'

'I gave him a drink of tea from my flask,' said Carl. 'And I asked him where he was going. He said to the village and he'd be all right if he could just make it that far. I didn't offer him a lift because I was going the opposite way, but he had to pass the care home to get to the village, so I told him there was a shelter near the gate where he could have a rest and I said I'd get hold of Maeve, as soon as I had my phone charged up, and ask her to pop down and see if he was all right.'

'You did,' said Maeve.

'Not for a couple of hours,' said Carl. 'I plugged the phone in in the van when I set off but then I had to cut up the tree and so on. Honestly' – he turned to Miranda – 'if I'd known he was really ill, I would have forgotten about the tree. I mean, what's a bit of a delay, a bit of a diversion? It just seems urgent at the time when really, what does it matter?'

'It had stopped raining,' Miranda said. 'And the day was beginning to break. It was less dark than it had been.

Robin went back over the gate into the road and carried on walking. He found the entrance to the grounds of the care home and the shelter, as Carl had described it, and he stopped and sat on the bench inside, and waited. To gather his strength. For the daylight to come. To see if the promise of help arrived, and brought something to eat and drink with it.'

'I saw him,' said Maeve. 'He was walking away down the road when I was coming down the drive to find him. He looked so lonely, so raggedy, and I thought of running after him but it had been such a morning, I almost didn't have the energy. If only I'd managed to get away sooner, but, of course, it was chaos in the home, what with the electricity being off and the windows all broken in the lounge by a tree fallen over, still lying there, some of its branches pressed up against the bedroom windows on that side. You can imagine what a state the residents were in, most of them having no idea why the light wouldn't come on and the TV wouldn't work, never mind the strangeness of the tree lifted up out of the ground and trying to reach them through the glass. I can't say some of the staff were any better. It doesn't help, does it, going on and on about what the problems are. You just need to work round it. Anyway' – she lifted her hand and brushed away a tear that had been travelling down the perfect arc of her cheek – 'it was at least an hour after Carl phoned before I could get away to see if the man he wanted me to help had turned up and, like I say, he was just off, down the road.'

She put her hand back in Carl's and he whispered: 'It's all right, precious, there most likely wasn't anything you could have done.'

'After a while,' Miranda said, 'Robin felt he might have the strength to reach the village, which was only a mile away now. He walked slowly, concentrating on setting his feet down, one after the other, pausing from time to time to lean on a tree trunk or a fence post. It was broad daylight as he went past the first houses and by the time he reached the centre, the shop was open. He had no money but the idea of something to eat, something to drink, was so tempting he stopped and leaned against the window, looking into the gloom of the unlit interior. His legs were shaking and it was almost impossible to stand, unthinkable to move. The door opened and a woman came out, with bags full of groceries. The wind caught the door before she was fully through and banged it back against her arm. She dropped one of the bags and apples, oranges, bread and plastic bottles of milk spilled out round Robin's feet.

'His legs began to fold beneath him and he could not be sure what his intentions were, in relation to this richness in front of him; whether he meant to pick it up and restore it to the woman who had bought it, or to grab an apple and start eating. The customer obviously suspected the latter, taking account, no doubt, of his physical appearance, not noticing, maybe, the condition of his health, and she swung the other bag against his head.'

There was a pause. I assumed we all understood, by this time, that we had been invited to listen to this story, and we had been chosen to hear it because we had each played a part in it. So, naturally, we all looked at Berenice. Berenice kept on looking at Miranda, as if expecting her to carry on with what she was saying, as if it had nothing to do with her. As the pause lengthened, Berenice said, like someone just becoming aware of a coincidence:

'I went to the shop that morning, but I didn't see this incident. What a shame! I like to think I would have given him a hand if I'd witnessed it, though as a woman on my own, I am aware of being vulnerable myself.'

Miranda closed her eyes for a moment.

'After the woman had gone, Robin managed to pick himself up and, by leaning on walls and hedges and lamp posts, to reach the house he had been travelling towards. This house.' We all looked round at the warm, brightly lit room, as if confirming to ourselves that this house was, indeed, somewhere where a man in the state Robin was in might feel safe. 'Only when he got here, it was empty. Locked up, and dark.'

Miranda had been watching her audience as she spoke, up to now, but at this point in the story she looked down at the hands in her lap, talking, as it were, to herself.

'I was meant to be here, but I had let the friends I was with the day before persuade me to stay another night. It would be dangerous to drive, they said, in these conditions. Then in the morning we heard about the power cut in the village and the roads blocked by fallen trees. Best not to set out at all, they said. Stay with us, where you will be warm and well fed, rather than going back to a cold, dark house with no means of heating a tin of soup. I didn't argue. I didn't know it mattered.

'I reached home the following afternoon. It was nearly dark. I went into the house and put the lights on, turned the heating up, brought my bag in. But, I thought, 'Before I unpack, prepare some food, I should check the garden for damage.' I turned on the outside light and stood on the patio, looking round for anything out of place. There was nothing to see except that the door on the garden shed was slightly ajar; I walked down to shut it in case the wind blew up again and ripped it off its hinges. I so nearly left it; I was so close to going back indoors, drawing the curtains, opening a bottle of wine. But I didn't. I went down to the shed and I found Robin.'

She leaned back in her chair and looked up at the ceiling. Maeve and Carl were still holding hands. Berenice was polishing the stone of a ring she wore with the cuff of her blouse. Solomon was staring at the fire. Theo was turned towards Vi; he touched her sleeve but she folded her arms and watched Miranda, steadfastly.

I was thinking there was only one question which remained unanswered about this peculiar evening. Why had Miranda waited five years before assembling in the same room all the people who had come into contact with this young man in the twenty-four hours before, I was assuming, he died?

'I'm so sorry,' whispered Vi.

'There's nothing we could have done,' said Theo. 'But yes, of course, I'm sorry, too. If only we'd . . .' His voice tailed away as Vi turned her head and he caught the expression on her face.

'He was still alive,' said Miranda. 'That night didn't kill him. When I found him he was in a coma as a result of having taken an overdose of paracetamol. I have no idea where the paracetamol came from. He had been told they could damage his liver further if taken in quantity and he did not think he had any with him when he left London. Somewhere between the time he got on the train and his arrival in my shed he acquired three dozen pills and, deliberately or negligently, he took them, washed down with some dirty water from the rain butt. Because he was in pain and forgot how many he had already had, or because he no longer felt as if safety was available to him and the pills were a way out, he took them all. With the untreated hepatitis, the pills damaged his liver beyond repair. He has been on the list for a liver transplant ever since. None had been found by the time last week when he died from multiple organ failure.'

Vi made a sound that might have been a sob; Theo turned away from her. Solomon looked serious and thoughtful, Berenice looked gracefully sad; so, now I knew them better, they would have expected someone watching them to describe them. Only now I knew them better, I no longer believed what I saw. Maeve got up and went to Miranda's chair, crouched down beside her and touched her hand. Miranda turned her head and leaned her forehead, briefly, against Maeve's auburn curls.

'Thank you, dear,' she said, and Maeve, the only one of us able to handle someone else's misery, got up and went back to Carl. I followed her with my eyes and found Carl was watching me. His is not an expressive face, but I think I understood what I was seeing there, and I looked away.

Miranda began to speak again.

'I will be honest with you, now. I do not know the truth about Robin's journey; he could remember very little of it – only an impression or two, a sense of being in one place or another, with one person or another. He was left with an awareness of the road travelled but no knowledge of the path the road followed. I have described it as I imagined it to be, not necessarily as it was. So I do not know if you have all been honest with me. If you have told me the truth, thank you. If you have not, maybe you have reasons, which may be important to you. Nothing in this life has ever been as important to me as Robin was. He was my son. And now he is dead and I have had five years to prepare for his going, but it was not enough.'

We all left together. Most of us stuck with the time-honoured formula, expressing thanks for the hospitality, as we went out of the door, but in a subdued way, in keeping with the closing notes of the evening. Only Maeve and Vi did not mention the lovely food, the interesting company, but murmured something more personal as it came to their turn to take leave of Miranda.

It was a relief to be outside, in the chill, still darkness. Maeve and Carl walked off into the night, hand in hand. I watched Vi walking ahead of Theo, her head held stiffly erect, neither looking at nor speaking to him as she climbed into their car. I thought the lives of this couple would be changed for ever by the evening we had just spent; the hollowness at the heart of the way they lived had been exposed, to Vi if not to Theo. Berenice, elegant as ever in a carefully placed shawl, lifted a hand in farewell and drove away, untouched, I believe, by the story she had just heard; lacking even the small seed of self-knowledge needed to allow her to confront her part in it. My house lay in the same direction as Solomon Thorogood's and, though I tried to slip off ahead of him, having no appetite then or since for his company, he caught me up and walked at my side.

'You know,' he said, when we were well away from

Miranda's house, 'that young man's death was the result of drug abuse; it was bound to be. He brought it on himself.'

Unlike Berenice, he understood what he had done, and he chose to ignore it. As – if I am frank – I had planned to do until that moment. But something broke within me as he spoke. A lifetime of playing my own game, no matter the cost to others, without fear or shame or guilt, had not prepared me for the feeling I had when Solomon voiced what I had been thinking, and I realized I was no better a man than him.

'He was the victim of his own weakness,' I said. 'But aren't we all?'

I have never regained my peace of mind.

THE WEEKEND
IN QUESTION

The village was called Scruton. It was an ugly name which was unfortunate, or ironic, for it was beautiful; the houses, mellow with age, faced each other across the village green like well-turned-out guests at a vicarage tea party, shielded from the vulgar gaze by the curtains of woodland that surrounded it. This was not the sort of place, everyone would have said, where murders were committed. On the contrary, it was desirable.

It was so desirable that none of the houses Henrietta could see from the front step of her cottage in Scruton was owned by anyone who lived there. To each other in the pub, or on Facebook, the owners claimed they did indeed live in Scruton, but were forced to spend time away because of the demands made on them by their careers, their children, their friends, their commitments to charity and to culture. On a Monday evening in winter Henrietta could stand on her doorstep, waiting for the dog to defecate in the garden of Field View Cottage next door, and know that no other lights would be burning in the houses, no cursors flashing on computer screens, no human lungs breathing in and out anywhere closer than in the cottage on the outskirts where poor, confused Mrs Eldred lived with a succession of carers, or in the pebble-dash terrace up a narrow lane leading nowhere, the property of the unsavoury Robinson family, though most of the tribe, these days, denied the Robinson connection. If Henrietta had needed help, as she stood on the doorstep, and had called for it as loudly as she could, none of the people in these dwellings would have been able to hear her.

She had been born here; it was the only home she had known. But as far as she was concerned, what had happened to the village during her lifetime was a good thing. As the only trustworthy person left living in Scruton, she was in receipt of more money than she needed from the other householders, in exchange for services they could not perform for themselves. Many of these were small: plant-watering, parcel-receiving, letting engineers into kitchens. But the compensation for these tasks was grossly inflated by the understanding that Henrietta would, in return, 'keep an eye on the place'. The owners understood that this was why they paid an hourly rate several times over the minimum wage for time not necessarily needed; Henrietta understood that this was their understanding. A few houses paid even greater sums for the privilege of having their floors mopped and their beds made up before arrival, and in these cases, the understanding on both sides was that she was doing them a favour, and the envelopes left under the vase in the hall were never mentioned.

Henrietta's social life was no one's business but her own. That there was no one around to take notice of whether she had one or whether she didn't was, therefore, a bonus. Her well-being – as she had frequently pointed out (not quietly) in the days when she shared her cottage with others – depended on peace and quiet. Now she had it. Bliss.

It was the Tuesday after a bank holiday. The village had been full, all weekend. Laurel Bashford, who lived in The Lodge, had had a birthday which meant that her age, for the next twelve months, ended in a zero – reason enough for a party, to the likes of Laurel Bashford. Not only this, though, but Cat and Conrad Monks who lived in Scruton Cottage (it was a peculiarity of Scruton that the largest houses had names suggestive of cosiness)

47

had married ten years ago, on the very same day. Henrietta had been alerted to these two events and their astonishing concurrence in advance, and had submitted to an additional burden of work for the joint celebration which, in the planning, moved rapidly from back lawn barbecues to a street party. Henrietta mentally deleted all the exclamation marks apparent in the written and oral communications of this change.

It was quite a weekend. The pub from the next village set up tables and a bar on the Green. Cherry Suchenskaya from The Old Vicarage, mother of four-year-old twins, provided a range of equipment, games and treasure hunts for the children – or her nanny, a skinny teenager, provided them. Henrietta regarded this girl as a co-conspirator in the business of exploiting the residents and had struck up a friendly, if not intimate (she didn't even know her name) relationship with her. Bart Graham from Sunnybank had negotiated with a butcher – 'the sort of chap I do business with' – to deliver a partially cooked pig on a spit, which Bart oversaw through the rest of its cooking time with the assistance of his wife, Thea, and such teenagers as could be persuaded to take part. Bunting was hung up by two ladies in floral frocks who seemed to make a living out of creating and installing it, which made Henrietta wonder if there were not easier ways she could profit from the absence of the other residents of Scruton than by cleaning their loos.

Every house was occupied for the weekend, even Field View Cottage, next door to Henrietta, whose owners were male and resistant to the lure of Henrietta's services, in fact were barely aware of her existence. She knew them as the Philip-James. These were the names she had heard associated with them, and might have been any or all of their first and surnames, or none of them. They never had parcels delivered or any post too bulky to fit through the letter-box, so Henrietta had no way of finding out. They never spoke to her, even to sound off about the dog faeces in their garden, perhaps because they assumed it was the dog walkers from outside the village, who turned up in their hordes on sunny days to take advantage of the many charming paths round about. Or perhaps because the turds and Henrietta alike were beneath their notice.

The street party went particularly well. There was almost no friction at any point during the long weekend, partly because, Henrietta thought, the mixing of the two occasions, the significant birthday and the milestone anniversary, meant no one objected to people they didn't know or didn't like turning up, in case these strangers were intimates of the other party. There had been some absences and then unsteady presences among the young; there was some vomiting but not in plain sight; a bit of flouncing and some tears occurred among the less solidly together couples. There had been weary looks and ironic remarks between joyless couples who had taken the decision to stay together. All this Henrietta noted in the time she could spare from fetching, carrying and washing up. She made sure to keep an eye on the whereabouts of the more untrustworthy (the Robinsons who claimed not to be Robinsons), and to spot where fun was being had in unfortunate quarters. Altogether, an enjoyable occasion. And a profitable one. Not only the extravagant payment for the extra hours worked, but a freezer full of good-quality steak and a couple of dozen bottles to be savoured when the village was hers once more. When the cars had all left. Which should have been now. This Tuesday morning.

Henrietta came out of her front door early and breathed in. She took her dog, a particularly stupid spaniel called Arnold, out for a waddle round the wood behind her cottage and waved to the Not-me-I'm-not-a-Robinson loading trestle tables on to the trailer behind his pickup. Watched him drive away. There was still a car parked beside the flattened grass of the Green. She looked right and left, expecting to see a distant figure striding across the water meadows to retrieve it. It would be unusual for anyone to have come so far, so early, but stranger things had happened. Maybe, thought Henrietta, one of the weekenders had decided to leave a car here and go back to London with someone else. In which case, it was parked in an inconvenient position, and not very neatly. It was the sort of nondescript car driven by someone who knows nothing and cares even less about cars; in other words, not the sort of car she recognized as belonging to a resident. She walked up to it and looked inside. There was nothing to be seen. It was none of her business, she thought, but without conviction. Was not everything in this village her business? If not hers, whose? She turned away, pausing to let Arnold lift his leg on the back nearside wheel arch. As she waited for him to finish – and he was never a dog in a hurry – she noticed that the boot lid appeared to be not entirely shut. It was hard to be sure, in the dim dawn light, but she thought there was a distance between the edge of the boot and the lid, a slight pout, which might mean she could insert a hand or a tool – a mop handle, for example – and prise the two apart. If it came to that.

It was her morning for The Lodge and she let herself in, began the process of restoring order to the Bashfords' so-called home: unmaking the beds she had made, loading and emptying the washing machine and the dishwasher, finding things left behind that would never be missed or wanted – flowers, magazines – and putting them into her bag. The party had celebrated Laurel's sixtieth birthday, she noted from the cards, a decade later than Laurel had led them all to think. Henrietta listened to Radio 4 as she worked, answering back to the voices. When she had finished, it was raining. The village was empty except for the car, the one thing left that did not belong.

She still had to clean Scruton Cottage, the home of the ten-years-married Monks, and The Old Vicarage where Cherry Suchenskaya lived. It was not about to stop raining. She borrowed a cagoule from the Bashfords' cloakroom and ran the hundred yards to the Cottage. Normally, it was an easy job, the Monks being the sort of people who did not leave much sign of their passage, but today it took longer to sort out than expected because an incident had taken place in one of the bedrooms that resulted in a pillowcase being ripped and quantities of goose down released. She ate lunch from the fridge, watching the lunchtime news on the TV. It was still raining. The village was empty except for the rubbish truck collecting the recycling. The rattle and crash of glass bottles landing in the bin was loud enough to startle the crows off the trees round the Green. The car was still there.

Henrietta ran to The Old Vicarage and found she could not get in. The shelter provided by the porch over the front door was insufficient and by the time she had turned the key left and right and shoved the door with all her strength, she was damp around the edges. It appeared that a bolt had been shot, from the inside. The back door, then, Henrietta thought, must be unlocked. She was wet by the time she reached it to find that it, too, appeared to be bolted from the inside. She retreated to the open-fronted barn Conrad Monks used as a shed and found a towel hanging on a nail which she used to dry her face and neck. It left her less wet but smelling unpleasantly of turpentine and grease. She rang Cherry Suchenskaya to ask what circumstances had left both bolts closed, and it went straight to voicemail.

On her way home she passed the abandoned car. It affronted her. It added to the dampness, the smell of old fluids and the frustrated attempt to enter The Old Vicarage, to produce in her something like rage. She stopped, allowing the rain to flatten her hair and drip between her chin and breasts into the front of her blouse, walked up to the alien vehicle and lifted the boot lid. It rose gracefully upwards at her touch and left the interior open for her inspection.

In the first seconds after the boot lid had come to rest in the upright position, Henrietta thought of two answers to the question about what was inside. One was a pile of old clothes; the other was a tailor's dummy. Even as she reached out to touch the hand-shaped, flesh-coloured object, she knew she would regret it. The hand-shaped object was not made of plastic. The old clothes were indeed clothes, but they were worn by a body that was not that of a living person. The boot was full of a dead body.

Henrietta stepped backwards. She allowed herself to notice that she did not scream, although watching *Midsomer Murders* had led her to assume this was an unavoidable reaction. She was absorbed, instead, in trying to decide whether to shut the boot, or not to shut the boot. The clothes on the body were beginning to darken from the rain, and whoever it was did not need access to air to breathe. She shut the boot. Walking stiffly, because her jeans were now so wet it was impossible to bend her knees, she crossed the road and went into her own house. She walked upstairs and changed her clothes. Hung the Bashford cagoule up to drip over the bath. Then she came downstairs and rang the police.

While she waited for them to arrive, Henrietta imagined how it would be. They would be concerned for her, thankful for her brisk and unsentimental reaction, pleased with her crisp, informed responses to their questions. They would want to know everything she knew about the village and its absent inhabitants. But it was not like that. Though they did ply her with questions. Why had she opened the boot? Why had she closed it again (it turned out the latch had caught, this time, and locked)? Why had she waited from twenty-five past three, when she found the body, to five past four before ringing the police? When she told them about the incident of the bolted doors at The Old Vicarage, they stared at her and said nothing. Then Inspector Bradley Rose, the solid, sensible-looking older of the two men in her kitchen, said:

'Did you ring the bell?'

'Why would I do that? I have a key.'

'But the key didn't work, did it?'

'Ringing the bell isn't going to make the door open, is it?'

'Not unless there was someone inside.'

'I've already told you, there is no one in these houses during the week.'

'Then how do you explain the front and back doors both being bolted on the inside?' asked Sergeant Martin Sharp, the younger, slimmer, less capable-looking of the two.

'I don't know,' Henrietta said. 'I haven't had a chance to think about it yet.'

She was beginning to wish she had disposed of the body without involving these men. She wanted her village back and it had begun to dawn on her that it could be a long time before that happened.

Bradley asked her for the key to The Old Vicarage and gave it to Martin, who left the room.

'Now' – Bradley leaned forward – 'do you know who the chap in the boot is?'

'No.' It had not occurred to Henrietta that she might know him.

'You're very certain. I assume you looked at his face and didn't recognize him?'

'No, I didn't look at his face. I've told you, it was frightening, it was raining. I wasn't going to start moving him around to get a better view.'

'You came home and had a shower and changed instead.'

'What is *wrong* with that?'

'Let me show you his face, then, and see if you recognize him.'

Henrietta braced herself. She did not want to go outside, where it was still raining, and where vehicles with blue lights and people in protective clothing were filling a space which should have been empty. But Bradley produced a tablet, touched a few keys and turned it round so she could see the screen. She was looking at a photo of a man who might so easily have been asleep if she hadn't known he was dead.

She did recognize him. It was one of the Philip-James. The older one. It crossed her mind to say she didn't, but he was watching her too closely and she knew he had noted her initial reaction.

'He's my neighbour. In Field View Cottage.'

'What's his name?'

'I don't know. I've heard the names Philip and James but actually, I don't know them.'

'You said you knew everyone who owns houses in the village.'

'Well, yes, I know who they all are. But I know nothing about this man or the other one except that they own the house next door.'

'The other one?'

'The other man who lives there with him.'

'His partner? His father? His son?'

'I've told you, I don't know. They never spoke to me. They never asked me to do anything for them.'

Looking at the photo, Henrietta realized she had never really studied the two men closely. If this photo had been in a newspaper, she might not have realized why he looked vaguely familiar. It was the rough-hewn face of a man a little older than she was, an ordinary face. Or maybe all dead faces are alike in looking ordinary, all animation and expression lost.

When she looked up Inspector Rose was still watching her.

'Do you have a key to Field View Cottage?' he asked.

'No, I told you. They've never needed me. I've never been inside.'

There was a flurry of activity outside the door, people coming into her hall and speaking to each other, as if this was not her house, hers to let people into or keep people out of as she chose. Bradley Rose stood up and went to the hall and came back to tell her they would be leaving her for now, but might need to come back and speak to her again. When they had gone, shutting the door behind them, she went to the window and looked out. It was not quite dark, but she was blinded by the lights on the cars and ambulance parked outside her house. As she watched, another ambulance drove towards The Old Vicarage, blue light flashing. She remembered that she had not recovered her key.

It was still raining later when she went out with Arnold. She led him to the back of her cottage, preferring not to let him defile the garden of the newly dead. She would have snooped round the village but there were still lights, still vehicles. For once, she could have stood on her doorstep and called for help and she would have been heard.

The next few days were eerily quiet, so far as Henrietta's contact with the police was concerned. There was constant activity but it did not involve her. Although she still had keys to most of the houses in the village, she was prevented from entering any of them by the presence of police cars parked on the Green. She wanted to be able to go in and out of the houses as she normally did, and planned to do, when the police were no longer watching. She had developed a little dialogue with Inspector Rose, in her head, in which he was forced to acknowledge that her superior understanding of what belonged, of what was out of place, had enabled them to solve the case.

She glimpsed, through the rain, cars she thought she knew driving past. Cherry Suchenskaya's, for example. One evening there were lights on at Field View Cottage and a bulky shadow that looked like the surviving half of the Philip-James. She wondered all night if she should go round and offer condolences but in the morning the house was shut up and there were no cars outside. She carried on leading Arnold elsewhere to drop his turds, though. Out of respect for the dead and the surviving.

The incident was made public and Henrietta learned that the dead man was called James O'Mahoney and his death was being treated as unexplained. There was no mention of where he was found. He was described only as a 'resident of Scruton' whose body had been discovered near his home on Tuesday. The item was accompanied by archive footage of the village and more time was devoted to the beauty of the place than to the passing of Mr O'Mahoney. Henrietta braced herself for the press to arrive, knocking on doors, pressing for information, but they never came. Scruton in the rain was not much lovelier than anywhere else, and the 'unexplained' might only mean some out-of-condition city type had dropped dead of a heart attack in a spot no one walked past very often. As Henrietta, in her bleaker moments, had thought might happen to her.

Then the sun came out and Sergeant Sharp arrived in a car and asked if she would be prepared to come to the station with him to help with her background knowledge of the village residents. The words 'station' and 'help' had an ominous ring but, in the bright sunshine of a glorious morning, the sergeant looked a bit like a fit but easy-to-control young man she had once enjoyed a relationship with. So she said yes, she was so prepared, and she put on a pair of shoes and climbed into his car.

'Have you asked the Not-the-Robinsons, too?' she asked.

'The . . .?'

'From Beech End.'

'Oh. We have talked to them, yes.' There was a pause while he looked carefully both ways before pulling out into a busy road. 'Why do you call them Not-the-Robinsons?'

'There have always been Robinsons in those houses and they have always been a certain sort of family. They still are, even if they claim they are not called Robinson.'

As he drew into the yard at the police station, he said: 'Capable of murder, would you say, the Robinson type?'

'No, of course not. What a silly idea.'

She was led into a room with three or four desks and asked to sit down at one of them, in front of a large computer screen. Inspector Rose, who also looked less challenging and more formal this morning, explained they had asked everyone from the village to forward the photos they had taken of the weekend's party. He introduced Henrietta to a WPC called Mandy who sat beside her and started calling the photos up on to the screen.

'Right,' she said. 'If you could tell me who the people in the photos are, and just a little bit about them.'

The pictures came up one by one, and Henrietta detailed those she recognized in each of them, looking at the figures in the background as well as the foreground. Among the first to appear were the entire Mabblewick family, except for Mr Mabblewick, who was presumably behind the camera. Henrietta had never known the first names of Mr and Mrs Mabblewick, who were both overweight and always appeared happy, which had led Henrietta to assume foolishness. Their habit of referring to each other as Mrs M and Mr M only reinforced this impression. They had asked her for help twice, once to be there to take delivery of an ugly floor-standing lamp, and again to supervise the removal of a perfectly lovely bird bath from the rear garden of The Old Chapel, the small and horrifyingly bijou conversion of a Methodist hall. Their two children, both boys, might have been discovered under any gooseberry bush, for all their physical similarity to their parents. They were thin and sulky and in the process of negotiating the assault course of teenage life, with the eldest now sprouting bristles and acne. His name was Ross and his wardrobe consisted mostly of trousers with crotches that hung halfway down his legs. His brother was called Oliver, and was less unattractive but even more sullen. All of this Henrietta reported to Mandy, but without specifying the bird bath which she now had tucked, tastefully, into a corner of her shrubbery.

The other family intent on recording their presence for posterity were the Finstocks from The Pines, an ordinary-looking house with one fir tree beside the gate. Sally, Aiden and their three little girls were captured in various poses, with the parents alternating so both of them appeared in one photo or another. They were perfectly groomed, dressed and graded as to size. Sally Finstock was the only person who ever asked Henrietta to do the ironing. Henrietta enjoyed ironing but was contemptuous of anyone who believed it to be necessary.

It was curious to note that Bart Graham, with his several chins and prominent stomach, was the subject of so many of the photos. Bart, wearing a chef's hat, and his wife, Thea, wearing a butcher's apron, stood behind the black and glistening pig. Even in the way he held the carving knife, Henrietta could detect the messy incompetence that meant nothing ever worked in Sunnybank, the Grahams' house, and an army of plumbers, electricians and delivery drivers was kept employed putting things right or replacing what was broken. Thea, with her long, stringy neck and dangly earrings, was borderline anorexic, which might have been a result of the way Bart threw his weight about, with its overtones of bullying, or it might not.

In the background of the Graham and Pig Show were people who happened to be there. In one, Cherry Suchenskaya's nanny was talking to someone just out of shot, only an arm and a fuzz of hair indicating someone was there. The nanny, who was young and angular, seemed to prefer the company of the children she looked after, Cherry's twin toddlers. Looking at her, frozen, on the screen, Henrietta noticed how pretty she was. Cherry herself, tall, confident, casual, was in many of the pictures, caught chatting to Mr Mabblewick, laughing with Stuart Smith from The Forge and his silent girlfriend, possibly French.

Cat and Conrad Monks, just ten years married, had chosen to pose with anyone else who happened to be in reach; Conrad, who was very tall, draping an arm round the shoulders of someone Henrietta realized with a shock was the dead man; Cat, who was extremely short, standing on tiptoe and laughing up at a man turned sideways who must be the dead man's partner. This was the only photo of the victim. His partner appeared in a later photo with the nanny. Partially obscured by the Finstock girls eating ice cream, he looked to be touching her arm or even holding her hand. If she had had control of the mouse, Henrietta would have homed in on the nanny's face because it looked as if she might have been crying. After several photos of people Henrietta did not know, the Finstocks, Stuart Smith and his possibly French girlfriend and Mrs Mabblewick appeared in the background of a picture of Laurel Bashford and her husband, Morris, standing in front of her birthday cake. Cherry Suchenskaya was on the edge of another photo of the cake and the Bashfords, looking towards Ross Mabblewick, who seemed to be walking past, ignoring the ceremonious moment. Bart Graham, released from the pig and the chef's hat, looked to be having an intimate conversation with Conrad Monks just to the left of a game of quoits; Cat Monks was talking to Sally Finstock, to the right of someone's dog, Cat looking smaller than usual in contrast to Sally's perfection. They were bent towards each other in a confidential manner.

So it went on. Henrietta was enjoying herself. She appeared in none of the photos; she took care to be out of shot when she saw anyone with a camera, and no one ever suggested that she should pose for them. And anyway, she had been too busy.

Mandy had a notepad on which she was writing down what Henrietta told her, but it looked a muddle.

'Let me,' Henrietta said. 'I'll do it.'

She drew a map of the houses in the village and put the names beside each. On the Green were:

Scruton Cottage: Cat and Conrad Monks, young, childless

The Old Vicarage: Cherry Suchenskaya, twin daughters, nanny

The Lodge: Laurel and Morris Bashford, middle-aged, prosperous

The Old Chapel: Mr and Mrs Mabblewick, large and jolly; teenage sons, Ross and Oliver

Field View Cottage: Philip and James

The Pines: Sally and Aiden Finstock, young, three little girls

Up a lane to one side and out of sight were:

Sunnybank: Bart and Thea Graham, middle-aged
    and fat (him), thin (her)
The Forge: Stuart Smith and French (?) girlfriend

Hidden in the woods were, at one end of the village,
the ex-council houses, and at the other, Mrs Eldred's,
which had never, in Henrietta's lifetime, been called
anything else. There were other properties, but these
were holiday lets, or belonged to people who seldom
came and had not been there on what Mandy kept calling 'the weekend in question'.

Henrietta was pleased with herself as she handed these
notes over. But Mandy's reaction was no more satisfying
than Inspector Rose's had been.

'You don't appear to know very much about your
neighbours,' she said.

Henrietta was taken aback. 'What do you mean?'

'I mean,' said Mandy, 'that you haven't mentioned
what they do for a living, or what motivates them, what
they care about. What they do with their time.'

'Of course I know all that,' said Henrietta, nettled,
'but there is nothing interesting to say about any of
them on any of those heads.'

'You think not?' said Mandy. 'Yet a man was murdered in their midst.'

'It will have been something to do with greed and
covetousness,' said Henrietta.

'This young woman, for instance.' Mandy scrolled

back to the photo of the Finstock girls eating ice cream with the surviving Philip and the nanny in the background. 'You only refer to her as the nanny. Don't you know her name?'

'Well, I don't. I know she's a good, sweet girl and she puts all the children's toys away before they go back to London, which is more than most of the mothers do.'

'So Mrs Suchenskaya refers to her as "the nanny", does she?'

'I can't remember, honestly. She probably uses a name but I don't recall what it is. Why? You must have found out from Cherry what her name is.'

'And another thing,' Mandy said, changing the subject, 'you've missed yourself and your house off this list. Are you assuming you are not a person of interest to us in this investigation?'

Henrietta stared at her. 'Why would I be?' she said. 'I was the one who found the body.'

Even as she spoke she realized that in the murder mysteries she watched in the evenings, Arnold wheezing on the rug beside her, it was often the person who claimed to have stumbled across the body who turned out to be implicated in putting it there.

Mandy did not reply.

On the drive back home with an unnamed PC, Henrietta reflected on whether she really believed what she had said about what lay at the root of the murder, or whether she had just said it because she was cross with know-it-all Mandy. It must be true, she thought. Greed or sex. They were obsessed with the first, these people, and she suspected more of the second went on than she could find evidence for. She needed her keys back so she could start her own investigation. Now she had another reason for finding out the truth: she did not like the idea of being a suspect.

At the weekend, the village filled with residents. None of them had let Henrietta know they were coming. She went over to the Cottage and rang the bell. Conrad Monks came to the door and looked down at her as if he could not, momentarily, remember who she was.

'Oh! Henrietta.'

'Yes, I just wanted to say, I haven't made the beds up because I didn't know you were coming.'

'Well, no. No one expected you to. Thanks anyway.'

Cat appeared in the corridor behind him.

'Oh, Henrietta,' she said, with much the same intonation as he had used. She looked less bouncy than usual, less of a perfect full stop next to the towering presence of Conrad.

'I'm here if you need me,' Henrietta said.

'Yes, yes, of course. We expect you to be.' Cat managed a smile, but it did not carry conviction.

Outside The Old Vicarage one of the Not-the-Robinsons was unloading logs from the back of his pick-up and stacking them on the porch.

'Hello, Dave,' said Henrietta. 'Is Cherry in?'

'No,' said Dave, lining up the cut ends of the last armful. 'She's gone to fetch her stepdaughter from hospital.'

Stepdaughter? Hospital? Henrietta was at a loss but not about to display her ignorance to a man in a hi-vis jacket and boots with steel toecaps.

'Right,' she said.

Next, she carried the cagoule she had borrowed back to The Lodge, where Laurel Bashford opened the door as soon as she knocked.

'Oh, Henrietta,' she said, just as the Monks had done, but Laurel sounded as if she had been disappointed in her expectation that her caller would be someone more significant. 'I don't suppose you have any idea what's going on, do you? No, of course not,' as Henrietta began to shake her head. 'Never mind.' And she shut the door, leaving Henrietta standing on the step with the hand she had stretched out to return the cagoule still outstretched.

Turning away, it struck Henrietta that what she needed now was an intimate. Someone who would exchange gossip with her in a way that is only possible if both parties to the gossip recognize they are essentially on the same side, and will not repeat to those gossiped about what has been said. Henrietta had no such intimates. She had never required one before, because the houses and lives of the village were open to her and she had not needed to hear someone else's point of view. But now.

She went back home and was cheered by Arnold's geriatric enthusiasm at her return. She felt, no question, lonely. No one came near her. By the middle of the afternoon she could stand it no longer and took Arnold out for a walk through a wooded shortcut to where old Mrs Eldred lived. There was no point talking to her – she probably thought the war was still going on – but it was possible her carer knew something. And there was no shame in asking the carer, who was of too little consequence for it to matter what she thought about Henrietta, or for anything she repeated to be taken seriously.

Mrs Eldred and the carer, a slender South African who showed perfect teeth when she smiled, were sitting in the sun on the patio shelling broad beans. At least the carer was shelling broad beans and Mrs Eldred was dozing.

'Sabrina, hi!' said Henrietta, fearing, the minute the name had left her lips, that this was what the previous carer had been called. Henrietta sat down and, taking a handful of bean pods, started to extract the beans.

'How's Cherry's stepdaughter?' she asked. 'Have you heard?'

'Lucky to be alive,' said Sabrina.

If it was that serious, Henrietta realized, the girl must have been lying, close to death, in the house while she was outside trying to open the door. Poor child.

'But she's going to be all right?'

'I suppose so. I haven't heard she did herself any long-term damage. Though you never know, do you? Depends what she took. If the police hadn't broken the door down when they did, she might well be dead.'

Henrietta pieced this together and felt a sudden flush of indignation at credit deserved and not given. If she hadn't mentioned to the police that she couldn't get in, they wouldn't have broken the door down. One dead woman.

'Do you know,' she said, keeping her eyes on the bean pods, 'I always thought she was the nanny?'

'Betsy? Oh, no! I think Mrs Suchenskaya let her look after the twins to take her mind off everything that's happened, with the trial and her dad being in jail and so on. She does like being with children; she's very good with them, isn't she?'

It had never occurred to Henrietta to wonder whether Mr Suchenskaya existed and, if so, where he was. She had imagined a divorce, probably acrimonious, with Cherry, who was tanned and slim and wore too many bangles, fighting to get more than her fair share of the loot, citing her need for a country cottage for the children as well as a central London flat. Henrietta wondered how Sabrina, who she did not believe had ever set foot in The Old Vicarage, knew more than she did.

Mrs Eldred woke up. 'Has the taxi come?' she asked Henrietta. 'We're going to be late.'

*

Henrietta did not have an internet connection. She had never felt she needed one. Now she thought she did. She drove to town and went into the library and searched for the Suchenskaya name on their public access computer. It was easy, given the unusual name, to find out that Sebastian Suchenskaya had been tried for, and convicted of, the manslaughter of his ex-wife. She had died in the kitchen of the home she shared with their daughter, Betsy, of whom she had custody. Sebastian, who was also in the kitchen at the time, had called for an ambulance, saying she had tripped and hit her head on the corner of the marble-topped island unit. Betsy, a third presence in the kitchen, had appeared to confirm the story and the police had appeared to accept it. But his ex-wife's relations stepped in with evidence of previous altercations between the couple in which violence had featured. The house was searched and the ex-wife's files turned up enough suggestions of her fear and loathing of the man who was no longer her husband to make an alternative scenario plausible, reinforced by bruises and abrasions on the body. Suchenskaya, the police now believed, might well have pushed or hit her, causing the fatal injury. The Crown Prosecution Service agreed and he was sent to trial. Betsy proved to be an unreliable witness, making widely divergent statements that either implicated her father or agreed with his version in some, but significantly not all of its details. The case had gone against him. He was currently in jail.

When Henrietta was younger and had gone to college, she had thought, for her first year, that she was having fun; she went to pubs, and parties, and was quite satisfied with the student experience. Then, in her second year, she moved in with some girls she didn't know, but who had a spare room available at the last moment. She realized then that she had been partying in the background, as it were. The real fun was happening somewhere else, somewhere these girls had been all along, swimming in the wide, wide ocean while Henrietta had been splashing about in the slick of water left by the breakers on the beach. It was too late to catch up. She resented the rest of her time at college for not being the experience she had thought she was having. So she felt now, looking at the details of Cherry Suchenskaya's real life, so different from the way it had appeared when viewed from her bins and bathroom, her fridge and kitchen cupboards.

Henrietta typed in the Bashfords' names. There was a link to a page for leaving charitable donations. Laurel, it seemed, was running a marathon in support of a charity researching childhood leukaemia, in memory of a girl unknown to Henrietta. Among the sponsors who had pledged money and left messages were the Grahams from Sunnybank; the message implied that the Bashfords and the Grahams had both lost a child.

Henrietta was halfway home before she realized she should have checked on the murdered man, but when she turned the television on that evening, he was the subject of a news item, because the police had announced that they were now treating his death as murder. They were appealing for information from anyone who had been in the village between midday on the Monday of the party and midday on Tuesday. Mr O'Mahoney was apparently fifty-two years old and a psychotherapist who specialized in supporting those with post-traumatic stress disorder. He was in a civil partnership with Philip Simms. The report had no more information on Mr Simms.

Henrietta smiled a little in contemplation of the avalanche of trivial and irrelevant observations the police would have to process, from people who only wanted to be able to say 'I was there'. As well as the partygoers, there would have been an abnormally large contingent of dog walkers, thanks to the good weather and the bank holiday. The report went on to show pictures of the village, in the sunshine this time, and the car, which the police would only say was 'central to their inquiries'. This was a police photo, taken in the rain, both the vehicle and its surroundings looking sullen and murky against the brightness of the library shots the producer had cut in.

Betsy Suchenskaya was not mentioned, but Henrietta had developed her own theory by the time the broadcast finished, and she would be surprised if the police weren't thinking along exactly the same lines. James O'Mahoney

must have been Betsy's counsellor. She was most probably the one who had killed her mother and now, racked
with guilt for letting her father take the blame, she must
have finally been able to carry the secret no longer and
had spilled the beans to James. Henrietta remembered
the photo with Betsy in the background, talking to
someone who could have been James. Horrified, he had
set off to find Cherry to tell her what Betsy had said, and
Betsy had chased after him and killed him. How she had
achieved this and how she had managed to insert the
body into the boot were details Henrietta needed to do
a little more work on. The overdose was her reaction to
the enormity of what she had done. Obviously. Henrietta was beginning to enjoy herself again.

It was the next Tuesday before anything happened. In
this time, there were people in the houses, but who,
and during what times, Henrietta couldn't make out.
It seemed to be completely random. One evening,
there were lights at The Old Vicarage; the next morning it looked to be shut up, abandoned, no cars in the
drive and the blinds lowered in the rooms facing the
road. The Cottage had two cars in the drive, which
never moved, but no lights were visible. Henrietta
could hear vehicles moving about and at first she went
to the window each time to see who was passing, but
it was often a stranger – dog walker or sightseer, who
knew? – and only occasionally did she catch a glimpse

of one of the residents. None of them came near her. She thought of going again to visit Sabrina at Mrs Eldred's, but that was not the way to test out her theory. Instead, she went back into town and researched Mr O'Mahoney and Mr Simms more thoroughly, looking for the connection between James the Psychotherapist and Betsy the Disturbed Stepdaughter. She learned nothing except that Philip Simms was a doctor. Nothing else. This screen was not going to give her the answers she needed. But she had no idea where to go next.

In the event, events turned up on her doorstep. That evening, the Tuesday a week after she opened the boot lid, as she was checking to see if the cheesy topping on her fish pie had browned enough, her doorbell rang. It was a particularly dark night. Although it was dry, the cloud cover was dense and there were no street lights in the village. Henrietta pushed down the switch for the outside light. Nothing happened. It was so long since she had used it, she had not even known it had failed. Peering through the glass panel of the front door, though, she could just make out, in the light from the hall, that whoever was outside formed only a small patch of denser darkness against the expanse of night beyond, so she opened the door. On the step stood Betsy Suchenskaya, hunched and pale inside a long-sleeved cardigan which she was clutching to her body, each hand holding firmly to the opposite sleeve.

'Hello,' said Henrietta, mystified. 'Is everything all right?'

Betsy shrugged, then started to cry. Henrietta had never wanted children because they failed to charm her and she could see no reason why her own would be any more appealing than those she saw playing on the Green, so she assumed she had no maternal instincts; didn't even know what this phrase was supposed to mean. Now, though, she felt a hint of something that was pity, as in the sorrow for someone else's sorrow, mixed with protectiveness, and this made her unaccountably want to hug the little waif in front of her. Such an action was beyond her, but nearly as uncharacteristic was what she did next. Stepping back, she said: 'Come in.'

Betsy followed her into the kitchen. Henrietta turned off the grill to prevent the fish pie from burning. She had a glass of wine sitting ready for her on the kitchen table but, looking closely at Betsy for the first time ever, she comprehended how young the child was. How could she have assumed this pale creature with its unbrushed shock of hair and bitten nails was a nanny? She moved the glass on to the side and offered to make a cup of tea. Betsy, it turned out, only drank herbal tea, which Henrietta did not have. Inspecting the cupboard for anything else to offer, she came up with cocoa, and Betsy, looking happier in the instant, offered to make it. She did this painstakingly, measuring the chocolate into the mugs, creating a paste with cold milk, heating the rest of the milk in a pan and whisking as she added it to the paste. Henrietta sat at the table as she did this, saying nothing. When the cocoa was ready, Betsy began to talk.

'I hope you don't mind,' she said, 'about me coming to see you. You won't remember but you were kind to me once before, when I was having a bit of a meltdown and you came into the room and just set about picking up the twins' clothes, talking about nothing much. Not nagging me about what the matter was.'

Henrietta tried to look as if she did remember, though she had no recollection of it and had never noticed the girl crying in her presence.

'I couldn't bear to go back to London and then I didn't want to be alone. I wanted someone to talk to and I thought you would be just the right person to be with. You don't get involved, do you? You just get on with your own life.' The tears had dried on her face, which looked even younger and prettier in the bright light of the kitchen.

'I suppose that's right,' said Henrietta.

'I wish I wasn't involved,' said Betsy, looking close to tears again. 'But I am. I really am. I can't help thinking it was all my fault.'

Henrietta shook her head. 'That must be difficult to cope with. But you may be wrong. Do you want to talk about it?'

And Betsy did. Hardly able to believe her luck, the

fish pie cooling under the grill, the glass of wine untasted, Henrietta sat as still as she could, not to interrupt the flow.

Betsy had been seeing James O'Mahoney, she explained, to help her with the trauma of her mother's death. He had been wonderful. It had all been behind her, pretty much. She was back at college, down to having sessions once a month, not having to take her medication at all. In the sessions, they now talked about the good things; about her twin half-sisters, her netball team. It was obvious to Henrietta, in the words and the silences, in the nervous motion of Betsy's hands stroking the sleeves of her cardigan and the constant eye movement, that this state of equilibrium, if not actual happiness, that Betsy was describing was fragile, at best; at worst, a lie constructed to hold the cracks closed.

This was all before the party, Betsy went on. At the party, she had been standing idle, waiting for the twins to have their faces painted, and Mr Mabblewick from the Chapel had been standing next to her, waiting for his wife to bring him another pork roll. Betsy knew who he was but did not remember having spoken to him before. He said to her, as they stood there:

'It won't be long before your dad comes out. I expect you're looking forward to it.' Betsy turned and stared at him and he laughed. 'Don't worry, I'm not making a study of your family. I work in the probation service and his case is being handled by my team.' Then he walked off, leaving Betsy with the unshakeable understanding that her life had just fallen apart. What it was that frightened her so much about her father's release – physical fear for her safety, never wanting to see him again because of what he had done, or just wanting nothing in her new, stable life to change – she did not say. But it was clear she had been devastated by the news.

'You'll be thinking I should have known he'd be coming out some time,' she said to Henrietta. 'But I didn't. I thought, after the trial, it was all over. James helped me believe it was all over.'

After the shock came fury, beyond her control. She was furious with Mr Mabblewick, whose broad, smug back was moving away from her, but mostly she felt betrayed by James O'Mahoney, who had encouraged her to think she was safe when she wasn't. She felt cheated, and she needed to tell him so; she needed to shout at him; she needed him and no one else. And at first, she couldn't find him. Her search took her away from the Green, round the buildings in the village, and at last, she heard the unmistakeable rumble of his voice. It came from the old blacksmith's workshop, attached to Stuart Smith's house, The Forge. It had been left open; tables and chairs, now in use at the party, were stored in it and would be returned later. The door was ajar and the sound of James's voice came from the dark interior. Betsy moved closer until she could see inside. James was sitting on an old sofa and Ross Mabblewick, he of the droopy trousers, was sitting with him – on his knee? Snuggled up? It was too dark, and Betsy could not tell. Without doubt, though, James had his arm round Ross and Ross had his head on James's shoulder. They did not notice Betsy.

At this point in the story, Betsy diverted into an incoherent assessment of her own character, the burden of which, so far as Henrietta could make out, was that she only ever wanted to be loved and needed; that she never put herself first; that it did not occur to her to resent ill-treatment, taking it as no more than she might expect given her lack of any attributes that would make her loveable. Henrietta thought this was a needless excursion as she had already understood the girl's low self-esteem and knew from experience that there was no remedy for it except the passage of time. Luckily, it turned out only to be a preamble to the explanation of what Betsy did next. It was, she wanted to convince Henrietta – or, more likely, herself – completely out of character.

She was so angry, she said, again and again, so angry. Henrietta thought she was not so much angry as frightened; the small, slight body of Betsy Suchenskaya hardly seemed capable of holding all the emotions her disturbed, teenage mind was feeling.

Denied an audience for her fear and fury, Betsy understood at once that here was an opportunity to punish both James, the purveyor of false optimism, and

Mabblewick, the bearer of bad news. She blundered back to the party and spotted Mr Mabblewick with his teeth embedded in a pork roll, laughing at the efforts of his younger son to knock over the inflatable skittles. She walked up to him and touched his sleeve.

'You should keep an eye on your other son,' she whispered. 'James O'Mahoney is abusing him in the old forge building while you're standing here eating.'

'What do you mean, abusing him?' asked Mabblewick, slivers of pork spilling out of his mouth on to the front of his T-shirt.

Betsy shrugged. 'Well, you know James's reputation. No young man is safe.' And she turned her back, as he had done earlier to her, and walked away.

'Was that true?' asked Henrietta.

Betsy, who had become quite animated in the telling of the story, began to cry again.

'No, of course not,' she said. 'He was in love with Philip.'

It seemed that sticking the knife (metaphorically) into Mabblewick had not cooled Betsy down, and she went round the Green looking for Philip. He was helping the smallest of the Finstock girls pick up the precious things she had been carrying in a little pink bag in her little pink fist, which had fallen out when she let go of the handle. Betsy knelt beside Philip and scooped up the remaining pebbles, fragments of shell and plastic hair slides.

'You need to keep an eye on James,' she said, in Philip's adjacent ear. 'He's having sex with one of the lads while you're enjoying yourself.'

They stood up and Philip Simms, now towering over her, took hold of her arm.

'What do you mean?' he said. 'What are you talking about? Where is he?'

Betsy shook his hand off and ran away. She wanted to be anywhere, now, except here, at this party, in this village. She pushed through the throng of people drinking, eating and laughing until she was clear of the Green, then she ran, literally, out of the village and into the woods. She ran off the paths, so well used by dog walkers, into the undergrowth, stumbling over bushes and brambles until she reached the deepest part of the wood where the trees' canopy kept out the light and the ground was soft with old beech mast. Then she lay down, curled into a ball, and cried. And, after a while, fell asleep. When she woke, it was late; past the twins' bedtime, Betsy said. It took some while for her to find her way out of the woods and back to The Old Vicarage and when she got there, she found her stepmother sitting on the sofa and looking glassy, an odd word but one Betsy thought about before choosing it.

'You know how she normally is,' she said, and Henrietta did: poised, calm, on the edge of a laugh. 'Well, she was still the same, only sort of frozen.'

For a moment Betsy thought (hoped? wondered

Henrietta) it was her absence that was paralysing Cherry, but she soon saw it was not. Bart Graham was in the room with her, still in the clothes he had worn for the role of the slightly comic pig-roaster. He looked disorientated, adrift.

'What's happened?' asked Betsy.

'James O'Mahoney is missing,' said Cherry, not looking at her.

'Missing?' said Betsy. 'What do you mean, has someone killed him?'

She was thinking, of course, of her malice, her deliberate provocation of Mabblewick and Philip Simms, stirring up hatred and jealousy against a man now unaccountably absent. A man who was important to her.

'No one has killed him,' said Bart. 'How can you think such a thing? No one has killed him. It's just that he has a condition and we're worried about him. Tell her, Cherry.'

Cherry pulled Betsy to her. 'It's all right, my dear. We'll sort it out, I promise you.'

'How can it be sorted out when James isn't here?' Betsy cried, and no one answered her.

Cherry gave Betsy a sleeping tablet and she slept until dawn when Cherry woke her to tell her to get up and dressed. They were going back to London.

'How can we go if James hasn't been found?' Betsy said.

'Oh, my dear,' said Cherry. She had not recovered her

normal balance; on the contrary, she looked even more fragile this morning than she had done the night before.

Betsy felt James's absence like the loss of a leg, like the loss of both legs. She would never, she felt, be able to walk through life without him. That he was dead was a conviction so strong she did not feel the need to voice it. So she didn't. She just rolled over in bed and told Cherry she wanted to stay for a couple of days. Wanted to be by herself. In the end, desperate to leave, with the twins squabbling in the hall and the car packed, Cherry gave in. She would come back in a couple of days, she said, and left.

Cherry, Betsy was keen to explain, had no idea how upset she was. She didn't know about the conversation with Mabblewick. Had she known, she would never have left Betsy alone in reach of the medication that had stockpiled as Betsy had stopped taking it. Cherry had also assumed that Henrietta would be coming in to clean, and would let her know if anything was amiss. As it was, the absence of James was too big a loss to contemplate, alongside the threat of having to meet her father again, and Betsy had bolted the doors and taken the pills.

'They were never going to kill me, anyway,' she said.

They sat in silence for a while, Henrietta sorting through what she might say that would make this scrap of a girl feel better, because the sense of ownership of someone else's grief that had struck her on the doorstep had not gone away, but it was not a feeling she was used to. She did not know what response to make. Betsy spoke first.

'It's always me,' she said. 'It must be something to do with me. First my mum, then James. The people I love, they don't just *die*, someone kills them. It feels like it's my fault.'

Henrietta, not quite believing she was doing this, reached out and took hold of Betsy's hand, felt the little twiggy fingers curl round hers.

'I learned long ago,' she said, 'that if something happens that shouldn't have happened, you can drive yourself mad looking for reasons why it did. Believe me, it is never one person's fault, and it is never a co-ordinated conspiracy and I don't believe in some malign god. What it turns out to be is a series of coincidences and accidents that ended up with this result.'

As she spoke, Henrietta realized that she did know this, but she had never articulated it before, and had never applied the wisdom, retrospectively, to the things that had gone wrong in her own life. Now, she thought that of course her current situation – living alone in the house she was born in and working as a paid help – was not entirely her mother's fault, or her ex-husband's fault, as she had always told herself. She had chosen to give up college to look after the first because she had hopes of marrying the second. Not just because her mother was a domineering, demanding woman, though she was, but because this particular man had walked into the pub on that particular day. Then the disaster that her marriage turned out to be was not wholly because her husband was weak, but because he lost his job, which meant he also wallowed in self-pity. And because he was embittered by her refusal to have children – she had had enough of those when her mother was still fit enough to fill the house with needy foster children. She felt comforted by the thought that, later, she would be able to contemplate all this more calmly in the light of what she had just said. Betsy seemed to find it calming, too. She wiped her face with the sleeve of her cardigan and got up to go.

'I knew it was a good idea to talk to you,' she said. 'You don't make judgements.'

In the hall, Henrietta asked Betsy how much of this story she had told to the police. None of it, was the answer. Cherry had advised her to say she hadn't talked to James at the party, which was true.

'And do you know now how he died, how he ended up in the boot of that car?' Henrietta asked, as she opened the front door.

'No,' Betsy said. 'I don't want to think about it.'

After Betsy had gone, Henrietta ate the lukewarm fish pie and drank the glass of wine, but absently, because she was preoccupied with the story the girl had told her, and in fitting it into everything she remembered about the day of the party and the subsequent days. In particular, she thought about the old blacksmith's workshop where James O'Mahoney was seen with Ross Mabblewick. It was out of sight of the Green, up a no-through-road that ended at The Forge, passing Sunnybank, where the Grahams lived, on the way. Henrietta had not been up there during the day, but as the party ended, she had helped Thea Graham carry trays of cooked pork back to the house. She could remember, now, wondering why Bart, ever the bustling busybody, had left his frankly limp wife to do this job, and then meeting him coming down from the direction of The Forge as she was carrying the last tray to Sunnybank's kitchen door.

'I'll take that,' he said, and almost snatched it from her. 'You get back to the Green. You'll be needed down there.'

Bart was habitually bluff and this had sounded more abrupt than it would have done coming from someone else, but at the time Henrietta had just felt pleased that the moments of glory in the sun with the pig and the carving knife had turned out to be hard enough work to make him grumpy. Now she wondered what he had been doing up at The Forge. She also recalled seeing Ross Mabblewick running, during the afternoon. This was odd, and must have struck her as odd at the time because she remembered it; he was such an inert, sulky young man that any activity was unexpected, but this was more than just moving, it was positively taking exercise. Henrietta tried to reconstruct where she had seen him running from and to, and had the impression it was from the direction of The Forge.

She thought about all the people who seemed to be implicated in whatever had finally happened to James O'Mahoney from when Betsy saw him in the blacksmith's shop up to when he had been placed in the boot. These people were Cherry, Bart Graham, Mr Mabblewick and Ross, and Philip Simms. There had been a point in the afternoon when the birthday cake was produced, exclaimed over and cut; at this time toasts had been proposed to Laurel and to Cat and Conrad Monks, and the festivities had settled down into a more relaxed, loose affair than at the beginning, when everyone had been meeting and greeting and the showmanship of Bart Graham had been at its height. Henrietta had a feeling that James O'Mahoney might have been missing before this point, but she couldn't be sure. She was fairly confident she had not noticed Philip Simms again, or only at a distance, outside the main centre of the fun, from shortly after the cake-cutting. Bart Graham had been there until quite near the end but – significantly, she now thought – not at the end. Cherry she could not be sure of, but she thought she had not vanished until most of the guests had left. Mrs Mabblewick and the younger son, she suddenly remembered, had been sitting on a bench while the clear-up was taking place, with even the always-smiling Mrs M looking morose. Her husband and older son had not been with her.

On Wednesday, Henrietta woke up with the joyful thought that she still had the key to the blacksmith's shop. Stuart Smith had probably forgotten she had it, as it was for emergencies only: when the stopcock needed turning off, for example, or the burglar alarm silencing, both of which could be done in this outbuilding. She set off after breakfast. There were cars in several of the drive-ways, but Henrietta ate breakfast earlier than most of the residents, and no one was about. There was no sign of life from The Forge, and no cars, so she felt safe in assuming that neither Stuart Smith nor his possibly French girlfriend was there. She unlocked the heavy planked door and slipped inside. She had no idea what she was looking for, but her original idea that she would be the one to solve the mystery by noticing what was out of place seemed even more compelling now, so she stood and let her eyes adjust to the darkness. She had not often been in this building. The burglar alarm had gone off unexpectedly only once, but she had been involved, over the years, in fetching and carrying the tables and chairs stored here back and forth to village events. These were all stacked neatly where they always were; she remem-bered having seen the Not-the-Robinsons gathering them up on the morning after the party. Apart from these, she would have expected to see an oil drum cut in half and mounted on legs, once used as a barbecue but now too rusted to be useful, and a quantity of junk left by the last owners which Stuart had never bothered to remove, including a wardrobe, two broken bicycles, a bird cage, a standard lamp and a sofa. It was all there, and nothing new had been added. Stuart hardly used this building, keeping whatever most men keep in their sheds in another shed in the garden, or using the services of men who turned up with their own equipment to do jobs round the house and garden, rather than keeping his own shedful.

What she did notice, though, was that the rubbish left behind had been rearranged. Whereas it had previously been all together in a corner, the sofa and the standard lamp had been extracted and placed more centrally. The lamp even had a flex trailing away from it which, following it to its source, Henrietta found had been plugged into a socket she hadn't realized was there. As she was bending over to inspect this, the door of the building swung open, creaking on its hinges as such doors are always meant to do.

'What are you doing here?' asked the man standing in the doorway. He had his back to the light and she couldn't see who it was, so she produced the excuse she had prepared in case Stuart Smith should prove to be, after all, in residence.

'I borrowed a couple of chairs after the party and I

couldn't remember what happened to them, so I thought I'd better check they were here.'

The man stepped further in, and resolved himself into the sturdy figure of Inspector Bradley Rose.

'Somehow, I doubt that,' he said. 'I don't suppose you'd like to tell me what you actually know about what went on at that party? And why you chose this particular shed to come and poke about in?'

'Yes, of course,' said Henrietta. 'Would you like to come back to my house for a cup of tea?'

'I would,' said Bradley.

When they came out of the blacksmith's shop, the village was full of police, some with dogs, forming lines and setting off to walk slowly across the Green and into the woods.

'Do you know what you're looking for?' Henrietta asked.

'Yes. Now ask me if I think we're going to find it.'

'Are you?'

'In my opinion, no. We've got a story, which more or less holds together, but no one will tell us if it's true. So we have to look for evidence to wave in front of the people who know whether it's true or not, to try and make them confirm it. Only, unfortunately, I don't believe the evidence exists where we can find it.'

'Do you think I'm one of the people who know whether your story is true or not?'

'No, I don't. But I'm hoping you can give me

confidence in some parts of the story. Then I can become confrontational with the people who do know.'

It was as Henrietta had imagined it would be, when she made the first phone call. The police sitting across the table from her, looking at her as the person most likely to help them delve into the detail of the events leading up to James O'Mahoney's death. Only, Henrietta felt more compromised now, more involved. Then, she would have said anything about any of the residents; she had believed them all to be people of so little basic worth, with their wealth and their carefully designed lifestyles, that real heartache, real tragedy could not touch them. Now that she had parts of the story available to her, she could see it was full of ambivalence and good intentions. She had to make a decision about what she thought of Inspector Rose and his team. What she said would have consequences and it mattered, all of a sudden, what those consequences would be.

'Right,' said Rose, 'how about telling me why you were in that shed?'

'I was looking to see if anything was different.'

'Go on.'

'Well, I've thought all along that if something had changed or been moved, or removed, or had arrived unexpectedly, anywhere in the village, I would be the one who would spot it. So I thought I should make an effort to look round. Just in case I saw something that might be helpful to you.'

She smiled at him. As she did so, it came to her that she might not have smiled at him on the previous occasions they had met and that therefore the lack of friendliness in his attitude towards her might not be entirely down to him.

'Tell me,' he said, 'did you start with the blacksmith's shop or have you completed a tour of all other buildings in the village accessible to you?'

'Actually, none of them are. I know I have keys but I'm not about to go in and out of other people's houses when they haven't asked me to go there for a purpose.'

'Or when they might arrive any minute and catch me at it,' she added to herself. There was an expression on Bradley's face which made her think he was aware of her thinking this.

'So what did you find in the blacksmith's?' he asked. 'Was anything changed?'

'Yes, as a matter of fact, something was. There used to be a lot of junk piled up in a corner and someone has used some of it to make a sort of snug. You know, moved the sofa into the open, plugged in the lamp. In fact, I've only just realized, there was a rug on that bit of floor, too, which wasn't there before.'

'Mr Smith might have set it up like that.'

'He might, but it seems unlikely. He's hardly ever here, and he never seems to use that building.'

'So who, then?'

'I don't know.'

'But you know something, am I right?'

'You must know more than I do.'

He laughed and leaned back, the wood of her kitchen chair creaking under his weight.

'All right, then. I'll tell you one thing I know, and you can tell me if you have heard anyone from the village mention this as a possibility. Mr O'Mahoney died from an insulin overdose.'

'Was he a diabetic?'

'He was.'

'I didn't know that, and I haven't heard any speculation about his death. But surely, this means it was likely to have been the result of . . . a miscalculation, or a mistake, an accident?'

'Exactly. But then why would those involved try so hard to cover it up?'

'Because someone feels vulnerable, or is trying to protect someone who is vulnerable?'

'Again, exactly. Now, will you tell me what you know?'

Henrietta thought before answering and, in the pause, Bradley leaned forward again and said, 'I'm sure you realize, until we have the story confirmed by the people who know what happened, we will not leave and none of those involved will have any peace.'

She recognized that this was true, and nothing that Betsy had told her implicated the girl in the final act in James O'Mahoney's life. So she told Inspector Bradley Rose the story, just as Betsy had told it to her.

'Thank you,' he said, when she had finished. 'Splendid.'

'Is it?'

'Helpful, certainly. I may as well tell you we believe Mr O'Mahoney died in the blacksmith's shop. And we know that a number of people had been in there around the time of his death. We have fingerprints and DNA samples and the question is, how far to spread the net in looking for a match.'

'Betsy never went in,' said Henrietta.

'No, we are confident she didn't. If I may say so, you seem to feel surprisingly protective towards a girl who, until last week, you mistook for a nanny and whose name you didn't know.'

'You may say so. I surprised myself.'

After Bradley Rose had left, Henrietta worked out that she did have a reason to go into at least one of the houses in the village, Scruton Cottage. She cleaned once a week for Cat and Conrad Monks whether the house needed it or not, and it was just over a week since she had last gone in, the day she found the body, when she had had to clear up all the pesky feathers in the bedroom. There was a car in the drive and the back door was open. Henrietta stepped inside and called out:

'Cat! It's me, Henrietta, come to clean.'

The Monks had always seemed the most anonymous of the residents. They were fresh-faced and unfailingly pleasant, and were bland in respect of their appearance, their behaviour, their furnishings. Their only outstanding feature, Henrietta would have said, was their disparity in height. Still, they came to the village more than most of the other householders and were therefore the most lucrative, for Henrietta, and had the best claim to being called local.

There was no answer to her call and she assumed the Monks must have gone for a stroll, leaving the door open, or were somewhere else in the house doing the crossword or discussing the best word to describe the colour of the peony in flower outside the window. She had come across them doing both these things, or something like them, quite often, and imagined this was how they passed their days – dreamily and to no purpose.

She extracted the vacuum cleaner from the utility room and carried it through to the hall, where she found something unexpected. Cat Monks was sitting on the bottom step of the staircase with a glass in her hand and a half-empty bottle beside her. She had clearly been crying. She was wearing what appeared to be pyjamas with what might have been chocolate ice cream spilled down the front. She looked extremely drunk – and the defining feature of the Monks was that they were never extreme.

'Are you all right?' Henrietta asked.

'No,' said Cat. 'No.' And she keeled over and laid her head down on the step on which she sat. 'I wish I was you, Henrietta. Your life is so organized. So right. You're a marvellous woman, I've always said so, a marvellous woman.' She reached out a hand and waved it about until it encountered the newel post, then pulled herself upright. 'No, listen, you should get yourself a decent job. Someone like you, why do you let us all exploit you the way we do? When you could do anything, if you tried? Anything! I wish I was you.'

It was news to Henrietta that any of the residents had an opinion of her that went beyond recognizing her usefulness.

'Would you like a cup of coffee? We could go through to the kitchen and have a chat if that would help.'

Cat wanted to talk – about her sense of ill-usage, her fury and her misery. It was clear from the start that these had arisen through some action of Conrad Monks's that Cat saw as a betrayal. She was the one who held them together as a couple and supported them as a family unit, never, never, NEVER throwing back in Conrad's face that he had failed to earn a bean in his life, while she had built up a business in floristry, going from one shop to five then to a franchising system that meant she no longer had to get in among the buckets and the Oasis first thing in the morning but could sit back and run her empire and spend time with Conrad while still making more money than he could have DREAMED of, and had never, whatever the provocation, hinted that his vaunted creativity that was going to make him famous and admired was so much HOGWASH, his paintings, etchings, collages, whatever other rubbish, were bad, bad, BAD. And now he had done this, in the face of her patience and tolerance and unstinting effort. How could he?

This plaint went round and round without ever answering the question of what it was he had unexpectedly found he could do. It was interrupted by Sally Finstock, who came in the back door as Henrietta had done, without knocking.

'Cat,' she said, 'how are you, my dear?' She was wearing a sleeveless dress in a shade of yellow edging towards amber, which caught the sun in its folds. There was not a crease or a stain on all its bright length and width. In contrast to red-faced, pyjama-clad Cat, she was a masterpiece of perfection. Even Henrietta had to avoid feeling dowdy in her jeans and T-shirt by hanging on to her scorn at the time-wasting represented by this level of cleanliness and order. 'Henrietta!' Sally said, noticing her belatedly. 'The police are looking for you.'

'Are they? Why?'

'They want you to go and sit with Mrs Eldred until they've arranged for Social Services to send someone in.'

'What's happened to Sabrina?'

'Oh, they've arrested her.'

'What?' said Cat and Henrietta more or less together.

'Oh, yes. They've just driven off with her in a car. Now, Cat, let's try and get you sorted out, shall we?'

Cat stood up and let herself be led away. Henrietta added smugness to her reasons for despising Sally

Finstock and went back to her cottage, leaving the vacuum cleaner standing in the hall. Sure enough, a
constable was waiting for her at the gate, ready to go
with her to Mrs Eldred's, where another constable was
sitting looking awkward in front of the old lady in her
grubby cardigan who had her mouth as well as her eyes
open and was giving no sign of being aware that anything in the room had changed, that the slender black
woman she was used to had been replaced with a solid,
pink young man she had never seen before.

'What is Sabrina supposed to have done?' Henrietta
asked the constable on the way.

'I can't tell you,' he said.

Whatever crime she might have committed, Sabrina
was an excellent housekeeper. Almost too good. Henrietta could find nothing at all useful to do in Mrs
Eldred's house. She made lunch, coaxed Mrs Eldred to
eat some, led her to the toilet, and, once the old lady
was dozing in her chair, took a prowl round the house,
looking through the rooms on the ground floor, clean
but cluttered, then the bedrooms above. The room Mrs
Eldred slept in was like her living room downstairs:
clean, cluttered, with a whiff of urine overlaid by
bleach. Sabrina's bedroom, on the other hand, was just
as clean, but sparse. There was nothing to show what
this young woman, displaced from her home country,
living with a companion who had no memory, no
empathy and no conversation, did with herself when

she was not cooking, mopping or wiping. No books. No computer.

Henrietta was about to leave the room when a mobile bleeped. Not her mobile. She felt in the pockets of a fleece hanging on the back of the door and found it. There was a new text:

> Pretend not to understand. Leave it to me. Sorry. Love you. Big C.

The call came from a number stored under the initials CM.

Mid-afternoon, Henrietta was relieved by a professional carer. She went straight to Scruton Cottage where Cat Monks was still sitting at the kitchen table, but fully dressed, with a cup of coffee, making notes on a tablet.

'Oh, Henrietta, where did you get to?'

'I went to sit with Mrs Eldred. They've arrested Sabrina.'

'Of course they have. I only wish we still had the death penalty.'

'Do you know what happened, then?' Henrietta asked.

'I know what Conrad told me. Though he's not trustworthy, as I now know. As you're here, could you do some tidying up upstairs? It's a bit of a mess.'

Henrietta wondered whether she should remind Cat about her advice not to let the residents exploit her.

'Not more feathers, I hope,' she said.

Cat looked up from her notes. 'What? Oh, that! No, I was only cross with him for vanishing for half the afternoon; it was a bit of fun. This is way beyond pillow fights. Don't worry, though, I'm going to be using financial weapons in future, nothing you need a vacuum cleaner to clear up. Can you just put things away, in the front bedroom and the bathroom? Don't bother with any of the other rooms.'

Upstairs, every cupboard and drawer had been ransacked and every item of male clothing, all vestiges of male-grooming equipment, had been removed. Henrietta restored order as requested. She opened the other doors on the way downstairs. In one of the smaller rooms, a single bed was piled high with what had been thrown out of the master suite; a mute monument to the fate of Conrad Monks.

Cat was still working. She had various bank statements and other documents spread around her and the wailing wreck of the morning might have been a different person altogether.

'Tell me,' said Henrietta, sitting down opposite her. 'What happened to James O'Mahoney?'

Cat looked up. 'Why should I?' she said. Henrietta wondered how she had failed to notice the pursed-up meanness in her little face. She had probably been looking over Cat's head at Conrad, the better-looking, more confident, substantially taller one. Cat had been there as an appendage, small in every sense. It would be trying to be Cat, Henrietta acknowledged to herself.

'Because I want to know,' Henrietta said.

Cat appeared to think about this.

'I really don't think it's my place to tell you,' she said, finally, suddenly sounding just like the bland little body she had always appeared to be.

Henrietta went to Mrs Eldred's in the morning, with Arnold wheezing along beside her, an excuse for walking through the woods. They were full of birdsong and brightness filtered through fresh leaves. It was a time for new life, Henrietta thought. And maybe not just for the birds and the trees. She needed to think – but not now. Now she could only concentrate on uncovering the story of what had unfolded behind the doors of the blacksmith's shop a week ago.

Sabrina was hanging sheets on the washing line.

'Thank you for stepping in yesterday,' she called.

Henrietta shrugged. 'No problem. Are you off the hook now?'

'No.' Sabrina put the peg bag down and came over to where Henrietta and Arnold were standing. 'I'm on police bail. My passport has been confiscated and I'm not allowed to leave the area. They haven't charged me yet, because they haven't worked out what to charge me with.'

Henrietta opened the gate she was leaning on and led Arnold into the garden.

'But did you do anything? Is there something they could charge you with?'

'Oh, yes,' said Sabrina. 'I killed James O'Mahoney. No doubt about that. Murder or manslaughter, though, that is the question.'

Henrietta had learned to look properly, over the last few days, to see past the shorthand she was used to using to keep people pegged as caricatures and, therefore, hardly human at all. Having learned this lesson, she saw that Sabrina was not just black and morose. She was beautiful and sad, graceful and emotional.

'I can't believe you meant to kill him.'

'No, of course I didn't. I meant to save his life. It's what I trained to do.' She folded her arms and looked at Henrietta, who said nothing. 'Oh, look, I might as well tell you the story. At least you will listen with an open mind. I'm not wrong about that, am I? You don't make judgements.'

'You're the second person recently who has said that to me.'

'Am I? Is it true?'

'I think it could be.'

'Come on, then.'

Sabrina went inside and checked on Mrs Eldred, then they sat on a bench outside the open lounge window; Arnold squeezed underneath for the sake of the shade and provided a snuffling, snoring accompaniment to their conversation. Henrietta sat at one end of the bench, holding herself into a still, tight package to avoid appearing to react when reaction was not asked for; Sabrina sat at the other end, loosely, moving her hands to touch the back of the bench, her knees, her skirt, even, as if forgetful of where they strayed, Henrietta's arm.

'You should know I trained as a nurse, at home in Cape Town, and I had a good job at a hospital there. Then I made a mistake and married the wrong man and I wanted to get away from the mess, make a break, so I signed up for this.' She jerked her head towards the window behind which Mrs Eldred sat, vacant. 'You seem to be someone who's happy with silence and solitude, so you won't understand what a shock it was to me, to find myself here where I can hear nothing at all except the sounds of the animals and the birds and the weather. I don't know what frightened me most: the loss of the noises I was used to, or the new sounds I had never had to listen to before. I missed everything about my old life but I'd signed a contract for a year and I had to endure.

'The only person in the village who noticed me was Conrad Monks. I knew why he noticed me, of course. I've met that type of man too many times before. But he was the only amusement on offer so I agreed to pretend I was in love with him; he's the sort that needs to think there are deep emotions involved, not just sex. We set up a little den in the blacksmith's shop. Stuart never went into it from one year's end to the next, so we felt safe meeting there whenever the purse-pincher Conrad had married let him come down here. I might sound bitter, but I'm not. I enjoyed the sex; even the play-acting was fun of a sort. 'It's only a year,' I thought.

'On the day of the party, he told me we had to have at least ten minutes together; he wouldn't be able to stand it otherwise, he said, so we arranged a time to meet. When I got to the blacksmith's at the time we'd agreed, James O'Mahoney was lying on the sofa, unconscious, with bruises on his face, and that oaf Mabblewick was ranting away at Ross who was shouting back at him so I couldn't work out what they were saying or what was going on. I went straight to James. His skin was clammy and his pulse was too fast so I shouted at the Mabble-wicks to shut up and tell me what had happened. Mr Mabblewick said something like "Stop making a fuss, woman. I only gave him a little tap." You know how men like him talk.

'Then Conrad arrived. He looked through the open door and didn't see the Mabblewicks, only me, bent over James on the sofa, so he rushed in shouting: "Oh, my darling, my darling, are you all right?"

'Of course, that set Mabblewick off. He saw at once what was between us and he began to have a go at Con-rad for being disgusting. Ross kept shouting: "Shut up, Dad, just shut up," and Conrad was trying to be digni-fied. I was the only one paying any attention to James. I felt through his pockets to see if he had any medication on him and I came across the card they give insulin-dependent diabetics so the emergency services will know how to treat them. It seemed to me he was suffering from hypoglycaemia, either because he'd injected and hadn't eaten, or hadn't injected. When they'd stopped shouting at each other I told the men to find Philip Simms. I didn't know he was a doctor, only that he was James's partner, but the others did, so they agreed he was the man they needed and Ross and Conrad went off to find him. Mabblewick stayed with me, babbling all the time that it wasn't his fault.

'Ross and Conrad came back saying they couldn't find Philip anywhere, so I asked them to phone for an ambulance. They couldn't have been more shocked if I'd taken all my clothes off or started speaking in tongues. No, no, they said, surely it wasn't that serious. Look, they said, there's a party going on; we don't want to spoil anyone's fun, do we? Of course, they were all thinking about how they could explain what they were doing in the shed, with each other, and me. About how James got the bruises on his face.'

Sabrina stopped talking and looked at her feet. She was wearing old trainers. Scruffy, cleaning-lady shoes.

'I knew what I should do,' she said, at length, 'and I didn't do it. I let them send Ross to James's house for a syringe of insulin. Mabblewick kept saying that was all it needed to sort James out, and he was bound to have some in the house, as if he had some real knowledge or experience. I wanted to believe he did, and Conrad was backing him up, saying, "Yes, yes, let's just get on with it," and Ross ran down there and came back with a syringe and I injected James and he died.'

She stood up and went over to the washing, feeling the edge of a sheet as if it could have dried in the fifteen minutes since she had hung it up.

'OK,' she said, coming back to the bench, 'you can say something now.'

'I don't think you're the guilty one,' Henrietta said.

'I'm guilty of something. Being weak, or stupid.'

'All right, guilty of stupidity. What happened next?'

'The place filled up. Conrad had asked Cherry Suchenskaya and Bart Graham to look out for Philip and when they found him, they all arrived together. Now there were even more people who didn't want to be caught with an unexplained dead body on their hands. Philip picked up the syringe I'd used and his hands started to shake. Whatever it was, he clearly shouldn't have had it in the house, or not in that quantity. Cherry was quite calm but she was adamant she wasn't going to be mixed up in it. Something about her husband coming out on parole. Only Bart wasn't just thinking of himself. I had him down as a complete idiot but actually, he really is full of good cheer to all, you know, not just acting it out? He was the only one who tried to comfort me rather than himself. Then Conrad realized I was the one who had technically killed James, and began to insist it had to be covered up for my sake and they all joined in, as if suddenly they really cared about what happened to me.

'So they hatched this plot. Philip was going to go down to the Green and bring James's car up the lane. The party was breaking up and lots of cars were on the move. Then they'd put the body in the boot and drive the car back to where it was. Philip had taken charge by now and the whole plan revolved around him. He needed to go back to London, to go to work first thing in the morning, so he was going to leave the car there, with the body in it, and come back up late the next night. He figured there would be no one around after midnight, and he could carry poor James into the house then without being seen. Then the following night, after work, he would come back in daylight and "discover" the body. He'd sign the death certificate and everyone would say how sorry they were and turn up to sing hymns at the funeral and then get on with their lives. We all agreed to it. At that moment, we would have agreed to anything as long as it meant we could go home and pretend nothing had happened. Only it didn't work. Someone opened the boot and found the body before Philip had a chance to move it.'

'It was me,' Henrietta said. 'I used to think I owned this village, no matter how many title deeds the so-called residents had, and there was this strange car where it shouldn't have been. I thought I had a right to investigate.'

'I wish you hadn't,' said Sabrina. 'Although, in a way, I feel better about it, from James's point of view. He was a lovely man, so everyone says, and he didn't deserve to be stuffed into a car and manhandled and lied about.'

'How did the police work out you were involved?'

'They were always going to, weren't they? They questioned everyone who was at the party to find out who had seen the car move, and who hadn't been in plain sight all afternoon. They narrowed it down pretty quickly and sat Conrad down – Cat in attendance, of course – and asked him where he'd been. Cat had already had a go at him for not sticking to her side like an obedient husband and he decided to act like a man (I imagine that's what he thought) and tell the truth. He told them he was with me because he was in love with me and he didn't care who knew it. I wish I'd been there to see her face.' She started to laugh. Henrietta had never heard her laugh before and it was joyous, so she laughed too. 'We were done for, after that,' Sabrina said, when she stopped laughing. 'He probably tried to wriggle round the details, but he'd make a rubbish liar, and anyway, they had a pretty good idea who else was involved by then so they only needed to talk to each of us and they'd get a different story. We never thought to agree what we'd say if it all went wrong. So, BAM! Over we all went.'

'What happens now?' asked Henrietta.

'I get deported, that's for sure. The only question is

whether I go to jail first or I'm straight on a plane. I tell you, I'm not going to miss this village. I know it's your home and you probably love it, but it's like living in a bowl of cold soup. You can keep it.'

'I've been thinking it was time to move on, too,' said Henrietta. 'I might as well have been living in a cupboard. I couldn't see out and I wouldn't let anyone see in.'

Inside the house, Mrs Eldred started to wail, calling out a name that was neither Sabrina nor Henrietta. Arnold, startled from sleep, hit his head on the bottom of the bench and began to bark. Sabrina stood up to go indoors, but turned back and gave Henrietta a hug.

'Visit me,' she said.

In the end, no one went to jail. The inquest verdict was death by misadventure, but Mabblewick, Philip Simms, Conrad Monks and Sabrina were all found guilty of failing to report a death and perverting the course of justice. Scruton, which for a moment seemed to have changed for ever, turned out, once the moment was past, not to have changed at all. So Henrietta left. She put her house up for sale and embarked on a career as a house-sitter. Having thought, once, she belonged in Scruton, only to find it had had its back turned to her all the time, she chose to avoid the illusion of belonging; jettisoned permanence for perpetual motion. It suited her. She spends the winters, the close season for house-sitting, in South Africa, visiting Sabrina, who was, as she predicted, deported and also barred from nursing. Undaunted, she retrained as a cook and set up a seafood restaurant, in a beautiful location on the coast. From time to time, Betsy Suchenskaya, skipping through adolescence and young womanhood looking for ways to avoid spending time with her father and stepmother, joins Henrietta in a house-sit, if she happens to be at a loose end and the location is convenient. It is from Betsy that Henrietta learns about the other residents of Scruton.

The Mabblewicks are still there, though Mr M lost his job and began to drink, and Mrs M's determination to stand by him seems to increase rather than alleviate his overwhelming fury at the injustice of it all. Philip Simms was struck off, sold Field View Cottage and vanished from sight. Over time, there have been hints of something unsavoury about the man woven into the fabric of the conversation among the residents who were there before the party (The Party). Conrad Monks has never been seen in the village again, though Cat Monks is still there, with a different name and a different husband, a man only slightly taller and slightly blander than she is. New families and couples have arrived to take up residence – following the Scruton tradition of never making Scruton their only home – in Field View Cottage, in Mrs Eldred's cottage and in Henrietta's old home. The waters of Scruton have closed over the place she used to occupy and no ripples remain.

*

Sabrina and Betsy have long since stopped suggesting they were responsible for James O'Mahoney's death, but, having spent time in the quiet of other people's houses thinking it over, Henrietta believes she has isolated the one moment at which the outcome became inevitable. It was when Betsy, having told Philip Simms that James was being unfaithful, ran away without telling him where to find his partner. It turned out that Philip had looked first in his own house and then come to the conclusion that James would have gone to a roofless cottage in the corner of a distant field where they had been together, in the past. So while his lover was dying for want of his care, he was a mile or more away, calling James's name and cursing him. This small, thoughtless act of Betsy's had changed so many people's lives. Not all of them for the worse, Henrietta thought.

A LIFE MEASURED
IN PUFFINS

When I first met him, I was eighteen and he was some age unimaginable to me then; over fifty, over sixty, even. It is twice the span of a puffin's life since I last saw him, the time it takes for an ash tree to grow twenty-five metres. I am over seventy now and he is dead, and for all I know, I am the only person who remembers his story.

The first time I met him he watched me in the mirror as I fluttered my hands round the back of his neck, tying the gown in place. I picked up the scissors, said:

'Just a trim?'

I was like a dancer, in those days, learning the steps by copying the moves others made.

Mr Chivers nodded and I began work on his thick, dark thatch. I was happier with the scissors than I was with the chat. The other girls eased each customer into a topic, and could pass the time without effort discussing holidays, children, the refuse collection, cake-icing, noise pollution. Men were harder to engage than women, and Mr Chivers's lean face and fixed eyes gave me no encouragement. I looked at his hands to see if they bore any sign of a man who cultivated vegetables. Vegetables had served me well as a topic with other men. I have his hands clearer in my mind now than any other part of him. You would imagine, after all the times I cut it, it would be the texture of his hair I remember best, the way it grew from the crown, the way it fell across his forehead, but although I have an idea of what his hair was like, I could draw his hands, if I had the skill, down to every last line, every vein, every discoloration. They were larger than a man his size should expect to have, and they looked like a pair of old gloves worn out with work; as if they had done wonderful service but were now spent.

That first time, I began to babble about the weather, about the way the newly painted walls looked in the sunlight. He interrupted me.

'Do you like stories? Shall I tell you mine?'

At once I said, 'Oh, yes. Please.'

'When I was young,' he said, 'I thought I'd take up flying, but after a handful of lessons, the school I chose went out of business and they sold off the planes. I went to the auction and bought one. It wasn't airworthy, as they call it. It was a single-seater, one engine, and it was being sold for scrap. No one bid for it but me. I hired a man to deliver it to my father's house in Scotland and I went up after it. After that I lived with him until he died, tinkering away to put the plane back in working order.'

As he spoke, his hands lay stiff and idle in his lap, but I could imagine them gripping spanners, wiping grease off shafts, manipulating engine parts.

'I had no cares all the while,' he said. 'All my thoughts were in the present, in the time I was living in, with my father and his needs, with the next repair on the plane. Every morning I woke up and thought, "What am I going to do today?" Not tomorrow, or next week, next year or for the rest of my life. Only today.

'Then my father died and the day after his funeral I cranked the engine on the plane and it fired. My father lived right out on the coast, no one close, moorland all about. I pulled the plane up to the top of a slope with his Land Rover, only the sheep to watch me, and I took off.'

My hands were still busy in his hair but my mind was with his younger self, a carefree orphan on a remote hillside, launching a homemade craft into the blue of a clear sky.

'Was it a fine day?' I asked.

'It was. I had so much common sense still about me, I wouldn't have tried it otherwise.'

'And it flew?'

'Yes, it flew. I remembered the mechanics of flying from the few lessons I'd had, but the sensation, the being connected with the plane and unconnected with the earth, I had forgotten that. But it was like living. As long as the plane flew, I was alive.'

'How long was that?'

'What measurement do you want? It was an experience; it couldn't be parcelled up into a number of ticks and tocks. It was long enough to be memorable. It wasn't long enough for me to wish it would end.'

'How did it end?'

'The engine stopped. I was over the sea but there was a dark smudge ahead of me I took to be land, so I set the plane towards it and tried to hold the angle of the glide. As I came nearer I could see it was a small island, maybe three miles across, rocky round the edge, wooded hills in the middle, nowhere flat to land a plane. But land it would, without caring for that. The sea might have been safer, but by then, that wasn't a choice I could make. In truth I hadn't many choices left, but there were a few. Do you know what it was I thought about, as the plane and I headed downwards?'

I shook my head.

'The safety harness. If I unlocked it before the impact,

I could be thrown out and killed. If I left it fastened, I could be consumed by flames before I had the chance to release myself and escape.'

'So what did you do?'

'I aimed for the best outcome. Land with it locked, unfasten it quickly. I practised unclipping the buckle, as the plane went down. Again and again. Shut, open. Shut, open.'

Still his hands didn't move in his lap, but I could see them as surely as if he had demonstrated the movement; grip, push, pull; and again, grip, push, pull.

'The plane came down in the canopy of the woods; it ripped its wings off as it hit, but ploughed on with me strapped in place, branches lashing me round the head and shoulders. At last the nose of the plane came up against the trunk of an oak tree, and the energy driving it forward turned into a spin. It spiralled downwards and I had my hand on the buckle so the moment the movement stopped I got it free of the catch and flipped myself out of the cockpit like a coin spinning to make a bet, heads or tails. I came down tail first, lucky for me. The other way up, I might not have survived.'

I had finished his hair, and picked up the hand mirror to show him the back of his own head.

'How long did you have to wait to be rescued?' I asked.

He looked at me in the mirror.

'You're in a hurry to reach the end of the story.'

'I thought that was the end.'

'No, it's only the beginning. The story is the life I led on the island.'

'How long was that?'

'It was long enough that none of the puffins living on the island when the plane landed would still have been alive when I left.'

'How long does a puffin live?'

'Twenty-five years.'

Then I asked him a question I never repeated but which is still unresolved in my mind.

'Is this a true story?'

He said, 'How much do I owe you?'

I asked the other girls about Mr Chivers and the island.

'Oh, yes, we've heard it,' said Bea. 'Complete fantasy if you ask me.'

'You're welcome to him,' said Dorrie. 'He can be your gentleman, if you like.'

He came in every six weeks, the time it took for his hair to grow long enough to justify my time in cutting it. Each visit, he started talking as if we had just broken off a conversation to fetch ourselves a cup of tea or close a window against a draught.

'I was lucky in more ways than one,' he said. 'The plane survived, too. It was left hanging in the trees until a storm knocked it to the ground, and by then I'd drained the fuel out of it, so it didn't catch fire.'

He talked like a man giving testimony, not the way my friends did, like I did, when we had a story to tell, taking care to give it drama in the detail, exaggerating the slightly odd into the extraordinary. And I became the judge, or the prosecuting counsel, wanting to know everything, teasing out the facts, making sure there were no gaps.

'Was that the first thing you did?'

'No. The first thing I did was run like a madman through the trees and the scrub till I reached the shore, and then I stood about on the rocks just as if I'd arranged to meet someone there and couldn't think where they were. I don't know whether I really expected to see help on the horizon, or whether I was just avoiding thinking about the future. When it got dark, I lay down and fell asleep among the rocks, and when I woke up, I went back to my old way of thinking – "What am I going to do today?" – and that's how it went on. Day by day.'

Each time he paused, I asked the next question, then the next, and he gave me the answers. I began to feel this was my story, something I was creating from the information available.

Q: What did you eat?

A: Berries and fruit, puffins' eggs and puffins, rabbits, mice and fish.

Q: How did you catch them and kill them?

A: With traps and knives made from parts of the plane.

Q: How did you cook?

A: In an oven made from boulders with a fire inside.

Q: How did you light the fire?

A: With fuel from the plane, twigs, a piece of broken windscreen and the heat from the sun.

Q: What did you wear?

A: Rabbit skins.

Q: Where did you sleep?

A: In a hut made from branches and plane parts.

Q: How did you wash, and clean your teeth?

A: In the sea. With a twig.

Q: What was the weather like?

A: Everything in its season.

Q: What did you drink?

A: Spring water.

And so on. These were the facts. How little they seem, but they filled many a haircut hour, plumped out as they were with detail. As he answered each question, I saw those hands, cutting, filing, trimming, grinding, moulding. I could smell his sweat, feel the sharp sting of a thorn catching in flesh, taste the hot, unsalted puffin flesh.

But the more facts I gathered, the more uncertain I became about where exactly the story lay. The more I knew, the more I felt I was excluded from the truth. As

I snipped the hair neatly round his ears with my scissors,
I asked:

'What did you miss?'

'You mean, what did I lack in my life on the island?
You don't ask what I was grateful to have, what I had
freedom from, only what was missing?'

'You must have missed something.'

'I missed being able to talk and have someone hear me.'

'And what were you grateful for?'

'Every mouthful. The sun when it shone, the metal
roof on my hut when the rain fell, the fire when it
snowed.'

'And what did you have freedom from?'

'Too long a list for me to tell you or you to remember.
Let us say, society. I was free from others' expectations,
from the need to compare what I had with what others
had. I did not have to pay tax, earn a living, find a
plumber, book a holiday, buy a car.'

I thought this over while I snipped.

'You'd have had nothing to talk about at the hair-
dresser's,' I said.

'Indeed,' he said.

I asked my mother what she would miss, if she were
marooned on an island. We were watching my father
play bowls, a game like a church service, following slow
rituals. My sister was expecting her first baby and my
mother was knitting, the needles clicking.

'Let me think,' she said, though her hands did not pause nor her eyes change their orbit between the game and the clock. 'I wouldn't miss the work, I know that. All the cooking and cleaning and running round.'

'But you'd still have to do that,' I said. 'You couldn't sit around doing nothing; you'd starve.'

She reached the end of a row and switched the needles round to start the next.

'Yes, but I wouldn't have to set the same standard, would I, if there was only myself to please.'

'How did you pass the time?' I asked.

'I wasn't aware of time passing. Each day I had food to find and cook.'

'Didn't you try and measure time?'

'Only in ash tree years. Each winter an ash tree would be half a metre taller than the winter before; half a metre's worth of extra fuel. The seasons mattered because the food supply was seasonal. The years only counted in terms of firewood.'

Bea wanted to know if Mr Chivers had told me about the rescue.

'No,' I said. 'I haven't asked.'

'What on earth have you been talking about, then? What else is there to know?'

'Do you know what I think?' said Dorrie. 'I reckon he was in prison all those years. The island's just a story he made up to explain where he was. After all, if it had really happened, there would be press cuttings, wouldn't there?'

Next time Mr Chivers came for a haircut, I asked about the rescue.

'You think you know the whole story now?'

'I don't think I'll ever know the whole story. But I don't need to stop hearing it just because I know the end.'

'Some people came to look at the puffins and found me.'

'Is that it?'

'What more do you want?'

'Did they write about you in the papers?'

'You want to read the story in other people's words?'

I shrugged.

He brought me a press cutting, pulling it from his jacket pocket with his huge, solid hands and passing it over, folded like a pocket handkerchief my mother might have ironed with tight, straight creases. I cut his hair first, before I looked at it. He told me how he'd plaited the shoots of old man's beard together as they grew, to form a solid rope. When the sap died down in the winter, he cut them from the plant and used them to tie logs together, to make it easier to carry them through the woods. When he had enough, he wove them into a solid blanket, which he used to catch puffins. He told me the best way to catch puffins was to startle them into taking off then cast something over them as they flew. They are not very good at flying, he said.

When I finished the haircut, I unfolded the paper. It was a short article, no photos, and the creases and various other marks had made some of the text illegible. What was left read:

MODERN-DAY ROBINSON CRUSOE

A team from the RSPB found more than just puffins when they went to a rock in the N*crease crease* to ring the birds in the colony there. They found Mr Robert Chivers *crease blot*ght pilot whose plane had come down on the island during a test flight.

'He was lucky we turned up,' said Ben *crease.* 'This is a small colony and we don't *crease smear* very often.'

Mr Chivers was taken to hospital but released after a check-up, none the worse for his ordeal.

'I don't know how long I was there,' he said. 'My *rip* stopped. I managed to survive on fruit and berries.'

He expressed his thanks to the *crease crease*-logical team and said he was looking forward to a *blot*.

I handed it back to Mr Chivers.

'It doesn't seem much of a story, for all those years.'

After I gave up hairdressing to raise a family, I used to see Mr Chivers in the street, as I walked past pushing a buggy. He looked ordinary, and I remembered what the other girls had said and I agreed with them. It was all a fantasy. It did not seem possible that those large, idle hands hanging out of the sleeves of his raincoat had done the things he said they had done. But now I am old myself, and I sit with my hands idle in my lap, looking at the veins and spots of old age, and I find myself remembering Mr Chivers's story. I wake each morning thinking: 'What shall I do today?' I occupy myself with what I will eat, how I will procure the food, how I will prepare it. I am grateful for every mouthful, for the sun when it shines and the warmth of the central heating when it rains. I miss being able to talk and to have someone hear me. I have outlived too many puffins.

BILL FLOOD

A grisly tale in three parts

I

STILL ALIVE AND SINNING

William Bloat

In a mean abode
In the Shankhill Road
Dwelt a man named William Bloat
He had a wife –
The bane of 's life
Who habitually got 's goat.
So one day at dawn
With her nightdress on
He slit her skinny throat.
With a razor slash
He settled her hash;
Oh, never was crime so quick.
But the steady drip
On the pillow slip
Of her life-blood made 'm sick.
A sudden awe

Of the angry law
Struck 's breast with a mighty chill,
So with careful art
And a contrite heart
He resolved himself to kill.
He took the sheet
From 's wife cold feet
And knotted it into a rope,
And hanged himself
From the pantry shelf –
'Twas an easy end, let's hope.
In the throes of death,
With his lastest breath
He said – nothing because of the rope.
He went to Hell
But 's wife got well
And is still alive and sinning,
For the razor blade
Was German made
But the sheet was Belfast linen.

I didn't much like Marina Blake when I first met her. But I didn't know her story then, and as the outsider in the place, it was some time before I found out what it was about her that made everyone else so sympathetic towards someone who struck me as so two-faced. I have led a peripatetic life and I have learned to observe, so I kept my dislike of Marina Blake very much to myself.

I met her at the Reading Group in a small northern town trapped on a coastal shelf with the sea dashing at it on one side and a range of hills isolating it from the rest of the country on the other. I had arrived in the place for a year's post as writer in residence. Various bodies in the town had come together with their separate pots of money, had written a bid or two and procured themselves this exotic pet, me. They understood none of its habits but were full of expectations from the ownership of it. At the risk of sounding arrogant, I would say they were lucky to have secured me. I had held four previous positions of the same kind, and knew the depths of their incompetence, and the extent of their unrealistic hopes. It amazes me no one has thought to write a crime novel in which the writer in residence murders the chair of the Cultural Engagement Committee in an imaginative way. But this has nothing to do with the story of Marina Blake.

I was invited to the Reading Group by Fiona Cartwright, the librarian; the library was, along with the primary and secondary schools, one of the institutions involved in my residency. I knew, from snatches of conversation I had overheard in these places, that Fiona had a son serving in Afghanistan, but I had heard no one mention this to her directly. No sooner was Marina in the room than she was speaking softly in Fiona's ear: 'I think of you all the time . . . hardly bear to watch the news . . .' Before I had turned round to look at her, I was already frowning. She was a lean woman in early middle age with hair that looked as if it had been styled with an egg whisk. Although I rarely saw her touching anyone, she had a physical way of interacting with them, standing too close, bending towards them, using her arms to embrace the space they occupied, reacting to what they said with exaggerated changes in posture. This was no reason to dislike her, I know, and nor was the character trait she exhibited most strongly: extreme concern for others. When the wine glasses needed refilling or the plates of vol-au-vents handing round, it was Marina who leaped to do it. She was concerned that Charlotte with the hip replacement should have the highest, firmest chair; that Sally with the bad back should have an extra cushion. I might have thought she was a warm-hearted fool, but it was too much of a performance; it didn't ring true. Her manner was a repellent blend of ownership and condescension.

My impression of her was reinforced when I met her on the seafront a few days later. I had a dog at this time, a terrier called Cass – short for Cassoulet. She was my third dog and I was working my way through the alphabet with food-related names. Apple had been run over and Brisket had died of old age. Cass and I had been in the town long enough to develop a favourite walk along the cliffs; the beach was shingle and hard-going, and Cass preferred chasing rabbits to chasing seagulls. I met Marina as I returned from this bleak and blowy outing and she made much of Cass who was, in fact, quite an ugly dog with a bit of an attitude. She did not justify being made much of and she did not respond to it with any gratitude.

'I'll take her for walks for you,' said Marina. 'You must have so much you need to do.'

'Thanks, but it's thinking time,' I said.

'Of course, of course,' said Marina, moving round so that she stood between me and the force of the wind, which was a powerful westerly. Had I decided to like her, I would have found this manoeuvre pleasing, but as I didn't, it gave me the feeling that I was being managed. She delayed me some while, letting me know that Charlotte was to be pitied for failing to stand up to a bullying husband. Sally's ill health, of course, was a result of holding down two jobs in order to fund her children's addiction to computer games. She was telling me all this, she implied, so I could be as understanding and sympathetic as she was when I met them again. If only, her manner seemed to say, other people were as strong and balanced as each of us.

'I'm looking forward to getting to know everyone better,' I said.

'I'm sure you will. I could see you watching everyone really closely. But I expect that's part of being a writer.'

Had I had hackles, they would have been raised.

It was a sad town. I arrived in a cold, wet spring and expected that the summer would be transformational. I thought the menace I saw in the sea and hills and the narrowness of the town's situation would become delightful aspects of a secluded seaside resort, when the sun shone, surrounded by opportunities to enjoy the world of nature. I was wrong. Although the tourists came and filled the hotel and the guest houses and laid out their towels on the beach, ate their ice creams on the seafront and their fish and chips in the cafés, the town remained dreary. The tourists were so much bunting hung on the walls of a high-security prison. The sun was like make-up covering pockmarked skin: the result was superficially more pleasing but at the same time a reminder of the essential ugliness it set out to conceal.

The broadband and mobile connections were patchy and slow and this was a fair reflection of the disconnected apathy of the local population. The people were like the place, or the place was like the people who lived there – which is not always true, by the way, as I can testify based on many 'residencies' in different towns. In this case, it seemed to me, it was. I wondered afterwards if this place, its situation and character, was a necessary part of Marina's story; if it could not have unfolded in such a way anywhere else.

The next Reading Group was at Marina's house. She lived in a three-storey Victorian terrace, near the sea. It was drab on the outside, but the interior was unexpectedly pleasant. Marina's style of dress was utilitarian with a dash of misplaced boldness – grey trousers, for example, with scarlet mittens in the shape of a cat. Her house was in quite another style. It was quiet, in every respect. There was nothing discordant or blatant about the decoration, the furniture, the accessories or the lighting. The room we met in was so pleasant I would happily have spent an evening or several evenings in it. Alone, of course. Marina was not altered by the setting. The soothing and the smoothing went on as before; the sotto voce conversations about matters too deep and painful to be spoken of at full volume took place in the doorway, in the hall, and around the side table where the wine and canapés were laid out.

I wondered if the rest of the house was as pleasing as this room, so I took a trip to the loo, further down the hall. I could see the kitchen beyond, and nipped in to take a look. It was as clean and tidy as the room I had just left; similarly uncluttered, well lit, comforting and functional. I had turned to go back to the front room when I heard footsteps descending a staircase, and I waited, expecting whoever it was to come down the stairs into the hall. But when the sound stopped, a door beside me, which I had assumed led to a pantry or utility room, creaked open. A figure stood at the foot of a narrow wooden stair to what must once have been the servants' rooms.

I had no idea of Marina's circumstances. I did not know if she was married, had children, lived alone or with any other sort of relative or partner. The woman who was now standing in front of me was hard to put into any of the categories of live-in companions it was possible Marina might have. My first impression was how indescribably unattractive this woman was. She was relatively short, overweight in a lumpy sort of way, had straight, coarse black hair and a pale-blue, tent-like dress which finished at her knees. Below its hem was an oasis of mottled flesh bulging over the top of a pair of pop socks. Her face was quite ordinary but it was impossible to look at it because of the awful attraction of a hideous scar which cut into her throat below her chin like a line of illegible text inscribed across her skin with a hard nib.

She stared at me without speaking and with an expression on her face that would stay with me for days, though I could not find the words to describe it. It was easy to say what her look did not convey – it was not cheerful, or friendly, but nor was it threatening. She looked sad, perhaps terrified, but she also looked – and this kept coming back to me later – as if she was pleading with me. I told her my name, and smiled. Her mouth made chewing motions and she produced a noise that was like a two-stroke engine chugging into life.

'Why, Ariadne,' said Marina, coming into the kitchen behind me. 'What are you doing down here? Come on, now, come on, that's right, it'll be all right.' She went up to the woman and took her elbow, urged her gently back towards the staircase and guided her to the first step. For the first time, I thought Marina's care was genuine, her gentleness unstudied. The woman, Ariadne, turned her head as if to look back at me, but the scar tissue impeded the movement.

'Sorry about that,' said Marina, briskly, opening the oven. 'You couldn't hand round these sausage rolls, could you? That would be very helpful.' By the time she had fussed with an oven glove and a serving plate, the moment when I might have asked who Ariadne was had passed.

A few days later I was alone with another member of the Reading Group – Charlotte of the hip replacement – in the primary school, gluing haiku on to a roll of lining paper to make a frieze round the classroom. Charlotte was the assistant head and had invited me to work with Year 6. I had introduced them to haiku and set them the task of writing these fiendish little poems – seventeen syllables, five in the first and the last line, seven in the middle; theme of nature; final line to take the reader off in a slightly unexpected direction. I like Year 6s. The children have grown out of being good for nothing much except being adorable and have not yet understood what a burden it is to be them, a realization that normally kicks in around Year 9. This bunch had been rather more stoical and reflective than normal, and had come up with constructions expressive of a downbeat view of life.

> *I have woken up*
> *to the sight of sunlight on*
> *dirty dustbin lids*

and

> *The scent of the rose*
> *is a perfume as strong as*
> *my dad's aftershave*

As we pasted and stuck we talked about the last book the Reading Group had discussed, and the next one. Then we fell silent. I am, as I have said, reluctant to gossip with any but the most intimate acquaintances, and I have few of those, having experienced the emotional pain that only someone who has knowledge of what you love, hate, hope for and fear can inflict. But I was also curious about Marina Blake; was I right to loathe her or were the people I had met right to like her? So I said:

'I bumped into someone in Marina's kitchen, the other night. At Reading Group.'

'You mean Ariadne. Yes, you don't see her very often. Quite a shocking sight, isn't she? Marina's such a saint, looking after her the way she does.'

Charlotte reminded me of a ball of knitting wool; chunky, hint of mohair. It was hard to imagine that under the layers of fabric and fat was an incongruous bit of mechanical engineering. I sensed an eagerness in her now, as she sat back in her chair and tucked the hair behind her ears. 'You must know the story?' she said.

'No, actually, I don't.'

I expected a story of banal, maybe comical, possibly ironic mishap. A bodged operation; a random accident with a fish hook; illicit sex too close to the cliff edge. The woman in front of me, the immediate surroundings of a primary school classroom with its colourful artwork and plastic chairs, the nature of the town itself, did not prepare me for the story she told. For it was shocking. Too shocking to reproduce in the breathless, excited way she told it, so I will stick to the facts.

Ariadne used to live next door to Marina, with her husband, Bill Flood. Bill was born and bred in the town but Ariadne was an outsider. She had come to stay with an aunt, and within six months had landed Bill and all the status that went with being the partner of the town's nearest thing to a celebrity. He was a wildlife photographer, winning competitions, credited in prestigious magazines. Though they had no children, and Bill was often away for long stretches of time, pursuing some elusive bird or beast, Ariadne seemed to mind neither of these things. She worked as a classroom assistant and was sunny, good-natured and well liked. But.

Charlotte leaned towards me, dropped her voice and spoke slowly:

'Something was terribly wrong.'

'What?' I asked, as there was a pause I felt needed filling, but it seemed it was included for the purpose of dramatic tension. Charlotte shut her eyes.

'No one knows,' she said.

One morning, it seems, Marina heard a noise she could not explain coming from the house next door. She worked – still worked when I met her – as a nurse in the local cottage hospital, and had just finished a night shift, arriving home about six o'clock when it was barely light. The noises she heard had never been described to Charlotte, but whatever they were, they were sufficiently strange for Marina to feel justified in using the emergency key she kept for the Floods' house, to go in and investigate. Did she not knock? I asked, and Charlotte supposed she must have done this first, but then she used the key. Luckily, as it turned out, because in the bedroom she found Ariadne lying on her bed in her nightdress with her throat cut, the pillow already saturated with blood and a steady patter of drips falling to the floor.

Marina set about stemming the flow and calling the ambulance on the bedside phone. The trick, she realized quickly, was to keep Ariadne still to prevent the wound opening further, and this she managed to do, holding her down on the bed, with a tourniquet as tight as she could risk it holding the two edges of the ghastly wound together. The ambulance took twenty minutes to arrive, and the hospital was twenty miles away, but Ariadne was still alive when she reached it.

The police, of course, came too, and once Ariadne had been bundled off the premises, they began the search for clues. They did not have to look far. In the cellar they found Bill, hanging from the water pipes with a bloodstained sheet twisted into a rope round his neck.

'He was dead,' whispered Charlotte.

When the incident was pieced together later, from the evidence at the scene and the account Ariadne was able to give, it seemed that Bill had risen early, perhaps with the intention of roaming the moorland round about to take photographs – it was a misty morning before a sunny day, Charlotte said. It appeared that he had gone into the bathroom to start shaving, and indeed did start shaving, with the cut-throat razor he always used, as his face was half shaved and half covered with foam when he was found. Then 'something must have snapped', as Charlotte put it. He went back into the bedroom and attempted to murder his wife with the razor he had in his hand. He was not by nature a violent man, and – this is all now supposition – he must have been so horrified by what he had done that he seized the bloody sheet off the bed and ran down to the cellar, where he twisted it into a rope and hanged himself. He failed to kill his wife because he had not sharpened the razor for some days and it was too blunt to be fatal. He was no better at killing himself. Neither the location of the knot nor the length of the drop was adequate to break his neck, and, according to the forensic evidence, it would have taken some time for the life to be choked out of him by the pressure of the sheet around his throat. If Marina had found him first, she would have been able to save him, as well as, or instead of, Ariadne.

It was two years since the attack, and Ariadne had recovered only slowly; the trauma and the wound had rendered her helpless, a timid invalid unable to care for herself. The damage to her vocal cords had left her unable to speak. But Marina had stepped in. She had moved in, caring for Ariadne as if this was her own disabled mother or sister or child. She had changed to working a permanent night shift so she could be there during the day to tend to Ariadne's every need. Nothing, said Charlotte, fixing her eyes on mine, nothing could be more selfless than Marina's devotion. She was close to tears, emotionally charged by the story she had told.

'Do you mind,' I said, 'if I open a window?' The afternoon sun was heating the stale air and the atmosphere in the classroom, thick with the smell of glue, ink and children, was oppressive.

'They're all locked,' said Charlotte. 'I don't have the key. But we can open a few doors if you like.'

We opened the door to the classroom and the one from the corridor to the playground. A breeze swept in and lifted the remaining haiku, scattering them across the floor.

'You have to admire Marina, don't you?' said Charlotte, on her hands and knees collecting paper. 'I mean, she'd known Bill since childhood, and she had been very close to them as a couple, but there was nothing to make her feel responsible for Ariadne. Yet she's put her life to one side and dedicated herself to looking after her.' She pounced on a floating poem. 'Would you do that?'

I had wanted to hear the story because my dislike of Marina made her interesting to me, but it was Ariadne I was thinking of now. What must she feel? I wondered. Did she wake each morning full of gratitude towards the woman to whom she owed each day? Was she comforted and sustained by the constant care Marina showed her? Or was her helplessness a torture to her, and the ministering angel an evil she was forced to endure? I smoothed out the rescued sheets and weighted them down with a pot of glue.

'I suppose Ariadne must be very grateful,' I said.

Charlotte frowned and selected another haiku to paste on to the frieze.

It is warm and dry
and the birds are all tweeting
'The forecast was wrong'

'I imagine she must be, but, you know, it's impossible to know what she's thinking. We did visit when she first came home from hospital but . . . well, it was hopeless trying to communicate.'

Ariadne, as well as having lost her husband, her self-respect, her health and her liberty, had, by losing her voice, lost her identity. She was visible only as an object of pity. I remembered the look on her face in the kitchen in what I now realized was her house.

Of course, the other question was: why? What had caused so sudden an outburst of extreme violence? But this Charlotte could not answer.

'I suppose Ariadne must have some idea, but, of course, she's stopped communicating.'

Of the people I had met in the town, I liked Fiona Cartwright, the librarian, best. There was a tweediness about her – not that she actually wore tweed (does anyone, nowadays?), only she had the rough-textured buttoned-up-ness I associate with tweed – but she had a wry sense of humour and straightforward attitudes. I used the library as the base for a number of my literary good works – creative-writing classes, poetry readings – and came to know her well. 'Charlotte told me about

Ariadne and Marina,' I said to her, a few days after the haiku session. I was in the library, watching her re-shelve teenage fiction.

'Oh, yes. Poor woman!'

'You mean Ariadne?'

'Of course. I don't feel particularly sorry for Marina. I know she doesn't have much fun, and she's given up a lot for Ariadne's sake, but you've seen how Marina is. I honestly think she takes pleasure in helping people, so it isn't a tragedy for her. No, it's Ariadne I pity.'

'She must be pretty isolated, from what Charlotte told me.'

'I think that's right, but she does come into the library, every Tuesday. She chooses five books at a time and she's read them all by the next week.'

'How do you know, if she can't talk about them?'

'Oh, we manage to communicate. I blather on and she gesticulates. It seems to work. She's quite a critical reader, actually. She can be very negative about the books she doesn't like.'

'Doesn't she write things down when she wants to communicate?'

'No,' said Fiona, 'no, she doesn't, which is a bit curious, I suppose, but Marina's always fussing over her so perhaps she doesn't want to hold things up.'

'I'd love to know what she thinks about, wouldn't you? By the sound of it, no one's ever heard her take on what happened to her.'

'You can't push, though, can you? If she doesn't want to "talk", in inverted commas, you can't make her.'

'No, but I was thinking, as part of the residency, we ought to run a writing competition. What if we asked for submissions on the theme of "Memory"? Then she can join in or not.'

'Give her a voice, you mean.'

'Exactly.'

'I like that idea.'

So we drew up the poster, and the entry form.

The next time Ariadne was expected in the library, I made sure I was there. It was just before closing time on a Tuesday, when the place was always deserted. Ariadne was wearing what looked to be the same blue dress as I had seen her in before, but also a scarf to hide the scar. Marina was carrying the bag of books to return, but managed to keep the other hand on Ariadne's arm, guiding her up to the counter.

'Here we are again,' she chirped.

Taking each book from the bag, Fiona talked to Ariadne as if this were a dialogue, only Ariadne's side of it was silent.

'What did you think?' (Thumb up and a smile.) 'Oh, good. I do agree; one of her best, I would say. Such a lovely, child's-eye view. Now, how about this?' (Thumb down.) 'I haven't read it. So you think I shouldn't bother?' (Emphatic shake.) 'I won't waste my time, then,' and so on.

Marina turned her back on them and asked me my view of the latest Reading Group book. I started to tell her, but, though she appeared to be listening, she reacted at once when Fiona suggested the 'Memory' competition to Ariadne.

'No, really,' she said, holding out her hand to stop Fiona giving Ariadne the form. 'She mustn't do that. It would be far, far too distressing for her.' Dropping her voice, though as Ariadne was only feet from her there was no chance she would miss what was said, she added: 'You have no idea how difficult it can be when she is upset.' Fiona looked at Ariadne, who turned away, and then at me.

When the two women had gone, she said: 'I think it would be a kindness to give Ariadne the chance to tell her own story.'

'I agree,' I said.

'After all, if anyone has a memory worth talking about, it has to be Ariadne. Leave it with me. I'll find a way.'

She was almost conspiratorial, pleased to be hatching a plan to let a little light into the life of a woman she liked, or had once liked in happier times. My motives were different. I was hoping that whatever Ariadne wrote would prove me right and expose Marina as more monster than angel.

Shortly after this, things occurred in my family that meant I had to cut the residency short and travel back to my home town. Almost overnight, Cass and I packed ourselves up and left. I was involved in my own affairs for a while and forgot about the sad figure of Ariadne in her blue tent, until Fiona, who had inherited the task of reading all the competition entries, sent me a letter.

'I'm enclosing a copy of something from Ariadne,' she wrote. 'There's not much of it, but I'm afraid it is very upsetting. I'm at a bit of a loss what to think. I haven't shown it to Marina; you'll see why when you read it. I have no idea what I'm going to do, but I know I must do something. I just have to work out what, and how.'

The enclosure was a small piece of lined paper, hand-written but so clearly that there was no risk the message could be misunderstood.

I am a prisoner in my own house and in my own body. I am bound to a woman I hate, who drove my husband to attempt murder and to commit suicide. It is thanks to her that I outlived him and I wish, I wish I had not. I endure because I am weak. The only help I need is what no one can give me – courage.

If I had an eggcup full of courage, I would kill myself.

If I had a mug full of courage, I would kill her.

If I had courage enough to fill the glass rose bowl Bill gave me when we were married, I would take back my life.

I have just enough courage to write this down.

I read Ariadne's words in a peaceful garden a long way from the sea, but as I read them, I could hear the pitiless dash of the waves on the pebble beach. The thought of the physical and emotional helplessness of her situation was a horror beyond imagining. Whenever I read of heroic rescues, of passers-by diving into freezing rivers or burning buildings, it strikes me how intimate and possessive an act it is to save someone's life. The saviour, I feel, must for ever have some rights over the victim. Each is thereafter part of the other's life story even if they do not meet again, or know each other's names. Ariadne did not have the luxury of anonymity. She remained at the mercy of her saviour through crippling injury, subject to a life sentence of perpetual obligation and subordination.

I stayed in the garden until darkness fell, reading and re-reading the few sentences. It was midsummer and darkness was a long time coming, but at length, when I could no longer see the words, I stood up and went back into the house. I punched two holes in the margin of the paper and clipped it into the ring binder where the other papers relevant to the residency were filed. Then I put it back on the shelf.

I I

THE BANE OF HIS LIFE

Bill Flood came into the world backwards, at the end of a labour lasting twenty-eight hours. This early failure to look life in the face was given lifelong significance by his mother, Mary Flood, for whom it worked as a definition, a motif, a philosophical creed in which lay all the answers to any question involving the word 'why'.

'I nearly died giving birth to you, that's why.'

It seemed to Bill, growing up, that it was his mother whose back was turned. Wherever she stood, she was facing away from him, towards the sink or the stove or at the window, where she would stand for hours passing comment on passers-by. If he had been asked, later in life, to draw one image to conjure up his childhood, Bill would have drawn his mother's wide back, the apron strings pulled tight and firmly knotted over a plain blue blouse. The sound of his childhood was his mother's voice; no actual words, just the constant rise and fall of sound.

Bill's father was a fisherman, prosperous enough to buy his wife a house on the seafront of the town where they lived, with a bay window from which to scrutinize the locals and the tourists as they went about their business. Shortly after his eighth birthday, Bill's father vanished from his life. This loss occurred at more or less the same time as the disappearance of a dog called Boo, and the man and the dog were henceforth merged in Bill's mind. Both of them were large and hairy and likely to appear at unexpected moments and greet Bill with physical enthusiasm. Both of them smelled of the sea; one also smelled of fish and the other of something similarly organic but less definable, and both these odours were at once attractive and repellent. As were their exuberant and bristly embraces. He never did ask what had happened to either of them, but found later that he knew – must have been told – that his father had drowned. Boo's departure was never spoken of, and Bill was left to puzzle over his last sighting of the wagging tail as it followed his mother into the shed where the chickens were taken when they ceased to lay any eggs. The chickens never came out alive; nor, he was forced to accept, had Boo.

After his father's disappearance, Uncle Fergus came to stay. Uncle Fergus was his father's brother and, like his father, was largely silent. He spent hours on a rock, whenever he came to see them, looking out to sea with binoculars, birdwatching. He lent Bill the binoculars and named the flashes of white wing that were the object of the activity, but Bill never managed to find the right focus or the right bit of sky until it was too late.

'I brought you something,' said Fergus, on this visit. 'A, you know, distraction.' He put a leather case on the table and sat back, lighting a cigarette.

Inside the case was a camera. Bill picked it up and held it in front of his face. Unlike the binoculars, which had failed to make sense of movement, this device clarified what he was looking at, simplified it into a composition. He loved it. He turned his back on the sea and trudged round the hills and moors inland from his birthplace, experimenting with photos of the most fixed and mundane objects: outcrops of rock, pebbles in a stream, the path worn through the grass by sheep walking in single file. When he knew what effect every change to the shutter speed, focal length and lighting would do, he began to photograph the elusiveness of a soaring skylark, a bee, a butterfly. His camera held still for ever the chaotic beauty of the natural world. At fifteen, he won a national competition for amateur wildlife photography and was interviewed on the local news. Bill was ever a man of few words and would never have found a way to express what he felt when he looked at the results of his work on a screen or in a print. He was surprised to learn that words were expected of him, when the picture said all that was of consequence.

As his reputation grew, the town became proud of Bill

Flood. He had pictures in *National Geographic*, the *BBC Wildlife* magazine, on television.

'It's good to see the effort I've put into that boy has finally paid dividends,' said his mother, 'and let me tell you, just giving birth to him was effort enough.'

Bill remained oblivious to his own success. In the wild places of the world where his skill was in demand, he expected to be thrilled by constant change, by beauty turning quickly to decay, or ugliness translated into beauty. He was alert for birth and death, for an abundance to be whittled away and for emptiness to be filled with abundance. But in the small town that remained his home, and particularly in the seafront house, he relied on constancy. Nothing changed. His mother's voice rose and fell, the blouses and the aprons were as they always had been.

Bill was not a man who made, or needed, friends and there was only one person, aside from his mother, who formed a significant part of his life at home. Her name was Marina Blake and they had known each other all their lives. She was an unattractive, skinny child who had grown into an angular, hard-edged woman; Bill was her only friend, as she was his. She was not a woman who was easy to like, and Bill – successful, uncritical, placid Bill – was her buttress against loneliness and lack of self-worth, and her hope for the future. She expected, in time, to marry him. The whole town expected it. It never occurred to Bill that a wife was something he needed.

Then Mary Flood died. She had used some of the money her son brought into her previously pinched life to go to Disney World with another fisherman's widow and her children. She came back in expectation of hours of enjoyment to be had from describing the outrageous clothes, behaviour and food she had met with in America, but on returning home, she felt unwell, a new sensation.

'I think I'll just go and lie down before dinner,' she told Bill, who was busy cataloguing his slides from a recent trip to Antarctica. 'Wake me up at six o'clock. The potatoes won't peel themselves and there's no point asking you to do them.'

At eight o'clock Bill became aware of the unexpected silence and tiptoed up the stairs. He stood on the threshold of her bedroom, a room he had not entered for twenty years, and stared in astonishment at the inert bulk on the bed. A blood clot formed in her leg over hours and hours of unaccustomed inactivity had detached itself and floated upwards to lodge in her lung, killing her quietly, not a word spoken.

When the funeral was over, he went back to the house and sat in each room, one after the other, listening. He would have said, before his mother's death, that he longed for silence, but now it had come it felt like an absence. After a few more days and nights in the empty house, he began to miss the physical presence of another human being. He had never thought of Mary Flood as company, but she was manifest, motive, as Boo the dog had been, or his father. He might have decided to buy another dog. He might even have decided to marry Marina Blake if Marina Blake had been to hand at the time. Unluckily – for everyone, as it turned out – she was away, doing a course on intensive-care nursing in Scotland. Before she came back, Ariadne arrived.

Bill was standing, as his mother had stood for so many years, looking out of the window in the front room, watching the gulls drift and soar and dive, when he noticed an almost gull-like figure on the sea wall, standing where he used to stand with Uncle Fergus. When she turned, he saw that this birdlike woman, or womanly bird, was shielding her eyes with her hand and looking skywards. He walked out, over the Promenade, to join her. Another man, approaching the figure on the wall, would have noticed that the impression of a gull had been created by the wind lifting a cream cape that Ariadne was wearing. Further, that she was far from birdlike, in the conventional sense of the epithet, but a rather plump girl wearing clothes that hung over rather than fitted close to her roly-poly body. Right up to their last minute together, he did not take in her physical appearance. He saw mankind as a uniform species that did not merit close attention.

'Are you looking at the herring gulls?' he asked.

'Is that what they're called? I come from Coventry. We don't have many gulls in Coventry.'

Ariadne was, in every respect, a plain girl, but her voice was beautiful: soft, low-pitched, on the edge of husky. If Bill had been attracted first by the gull-like cape, he was seduced beyond saving by the voice.

'I live just over there,' he said. 'Would you like a cup of tea?'

By the time Marina Blake came back a year later, she found the gap left in Bill's life by his mother's death had been filled by a lump of a woman with poor dress sense and a voice that was somewhere between a whisper and a song.

Ariadne perfectly filled the void Bill's mother had left. His delight in the melody of her talking did not diminish with familiarity, though, once he had secured her promise to love and hold him until death, he no longer bothered to listen to the words she said. It was enough that she said them. He was a man who had learned early in life to ask no questions, which released him from the need to listen for answers. Ariadne, whose love for Bill Flood was like a pain that never left her – unignorable and frightening – found soon enough that her questions went unanswered. If he did not want to answer questions, she would ask none. Instead, she made statements and waited for a reaction.

'I think we'll have fish tonight. I'll nip over to the fishmonger and see if there's any fresh cod. I can make a parsley sauce.'

'My mother did a lovely fish pie.'

'Fish pie! Good idea! We'll have that.'

For the first year of their married life, they settled round each other like animals circling in the grass to make a nest.

As this first year came to an end, Bill was surprised to meet Marina coming out of the front door of the house next to his.

'Don't worry,' she said, putting a hand on his arm. 'I'm not stalking you. I've moved in with Mrs Carmichael – she needs a bit of companionship, and a little bit of physical help, and I need somewhere to live, so here I am!'

'That's nice,' said Bill.

He left for a trip to Brazil and was away for six weeks. When he came back, he found that the two women had become friends. Marina was sitting beside Ariadne in the front room when he came downstairs the next morning. A landscape of patterned fabric was spread across the table and Ariadne was busy with a sewing machine he had never seen before, while Marina, with thimble, needle and thread, was briskly hemming.

'I was just telling Ariadne,' she said, 'how the red velvet curtains and the pelmets put me in mind of your mother. They made the house *hers*, if you know what I mean.'

Bill looked from the bare windows to the muted floral

fabric the two women were sewing. It was as if some trick of the light or temporary disturbance of his vision had momentarily obscured the red velvet. It was real; the floral fabric was not. He had not been aware that Ariadne was making changes to the house but that evening, as they ate their supper at the kitchen table, he noticed something else.

'The calendar has gone,' he said. She smiled.

'It was five years out of date, my love. I threw it away. I thought you'd just never got round to it.'

'My mother liked the picture.'

'Oh, I'm sorry. I didn't think you'd be particularly partial to it. I mean . . . kittens in a wellington boot! I didn't think you'd want to keep it.'

'No, of course not,' and he smiled back at her, soothed by the soft voice and the reassuring presence of a woman in the chair where his mother used to sit.

Marina asked him to come in and unblock the drain in Mrs Carmichael's kitchen. As he worked to loosen the fastenings on the U-bend she said:

'I couldn't help noticing how shocked you were by the curtain material Ariadne chose. You know, I did tell her you might prefer something darker, more like the old curtains, but she wants to brighten the place up for you.'

'I'll get used to them,' said Bill, his voice muffled by the cupboard.

'Yes, of course you will. And all the other things she's

changed. But still, I hope she respects your mother's memory.'

Bill went home and looked more closely at the house he lived in. He was surprised to find that, as Marina had implied, much had been modified without him noticing: walls repainted, soft pastels covering over the cream he had known all his life; new plates, mugs. He had been used to a house of creams, browns, dark red. He was living in a house of eau de Nil, rose, apricot.

'You've made a few changes round here,' he said to Ariadne.

'Not without telling you first, Bill,' she said. He could not know if this were true; he listened to so few of the words she spoke. He felt a tremor of unease; the first realization that this presence he had welcomed was, after all, a stranger.

He left again for Tibet and this time, when he returned, he looked for changes over Ariadne's head as she walked into his embrace.

'That bowl's new,' he said.

She laughed. 'Not so new, now, Bill. You bought it for me on our honeymoon, don't you remember? I've only just worked out where was the best place to put it.'

Wrong-footed, he stayed silent about the other replacements he noticed: washing-up bowl, laundry basket, tea towels.

'I know you find it hard to accept all the changes,'

whispered Marina as he dug over a patch of Mrs Carmichael's garden so Marina could grow lettuces, 'but, you know, she's so much in love with you she's just trying to make the place cheerful.'

'I rather wish she wouldn't,' said Bill.

'I know that, and I did warn her. You must let her know if you don't like what she's doing.'

That evening, as he opened the door to the cupboard in their room, he said: 'I don't like this colour.'

'Oh!' said Ariadne. 'It's the blue of the sky, and you've told me you love the colour of the sky.'

He remembered their first Christmas, when Ariadne had brought a Christmas tree into the house. He had tried to explain to her then how he felt about the intrusion of some debased version of nature into the essentially artificial world of indoors.

'The sky, yes,' said Bill. 'The sky is the colour the sky should be. This door should be brown, like it always has been.'

'Well, I wish you'd said that when I told you what I was going to do,' said Ariadne. For the first time, her voice had a peevish edge which moved it closer to the register of his mother's voice. 'I'll change it. I could strip it to the wood, perhaps. That would be more natural.'

'No,' said Bill. 'It's changed once. Best leave it as it is.'

Things started to vanish.

'There used to be a picture at the top of the stairs.'

'Marina said you'd always hated it, so I put it in the loft. I can get it down again.'

As he carried the bags of groceries into Mrs Carmichael's hall he repeated this to Marina. 'Ariadne says you told her I didn't like the painting at the top of the stairs.'

'Which painting, Bill?'

'The bowl of roses. On the landing.'

'Oh, yes. I noticed Ariadne had taken it down. I suppose she didn't know how much your mother loved it. I didn't tell her you hated it. I didn't know you did.'

Bill had had no opinion on the picture, just as he had had no opinion on the colour scheme or the curtains or the calendar. He had not needed to have opinions because these things were etched into the house, unalterable.

He did not mention to Ariadne that Marina had denied the remark about the picture. But the next time Ariadne used Marina's name as an excuse for a change ('Marina said you'd never liked that mirror') he checked again with Marina. He knew Marina so much better than he knew Ariadne. He could still be glad of the melodious sound of his wife's voice and the comforting flutter of her loose clothing on the edge of his vision, but she was not as familiar to him as Marina was.

'I never said that,' Marina told him. 'Why would I? I've never even thought about it.'

'That's what she said.'

They were weeding the lettuces, which were coming along nicely in the fine tilth Bill had created for them.

'I'm sorry to have to say this,' said Marina, 'but I do begin to suspect that Ariadne is determined to blot out every trace of the life you led before you met her. I can sort of understand it, I suppose. She can't feel secure in your house until she's made it hers.'

'I'm going to tell her to stop.'

'Oh, no, I wouldn't do that. It might make her feel insecure. And, after all, do you mind so much?'

'I don't like change, Marina.'

'No, of course. I'll tell you what' – she stood up and brushed the soil from her knees – 'I'll mention it to her. Tell her I know she means it for the best but you find it upsetting.'

But the next time Bill came back, from Indonesia, the old red patterned rug in the hall had gone. It was as if he had stepped over the threshold into someone else's home. Ariadne was out but Marina was sunbathing in Mrs Carmichael's garden.

'She's taken the rug away.'

Marina lifted her sunglasses on to the top of her head. 'I'm sorry, Bill, but I think she is honestly set on stripping the whole place of everything you've ever found familiar.'

'I don't know what to do.'

Marina touched his hand.

'I can't tell you, I'm afraid.'

When Ariadne came home, she said: 'I wasn't expecting you or I wouldn't have gone out.'

'I phoned,' he said. 'Left a message.'

'I didn't get it.' She looked shifty, he thought. Uneasy.

'You've taken the rug out of the hall.'

'I'm so sorry,' she said, and started to cry. 'I try so hard to do what will please you but I don't seem to get it right. I'm trying to make the house a lovely place for you to come home to.'

'It was a home before you moved in,' he said. He disliked tears.

'I don't know how everything has started to go wrong,' she said, searching in her cardigan pocket for a tissue. 'To begin with, I thought you agreed with me about brightening the place up, then you got cross and I was going to stop but Marina kept pointing out things she thought you'd like me to do, so I did them.'

'That's a lie,' he shouted. 'Marina has been telling you to stop!'

Ariadne took the sodden tissue from her face and stared at him. 'Is that what she says?'

'It's the truth.'

She took a step towards him and he took a step back.

'It is possible,' she said, 'is it not, that she might be the one who is lying.'

'Of course she isn't.'

'How can you be so sure?'

'She has never lied to me before and I've known her all my life. There's no reason why she should.'

'There's no reason why I would, either.'

'You want your own way. You want to change everything to suit yourself and when I challenge you, you
blame someone else.'

'Oh, Bill, Bill!' She turned away from him and lifted
the top of the rubbish bin, dropped the tissue in. The
bin closed with a sharp sound and Bill looked at it. It
was white. Metal. He could clearly see his mother's back
turned, as Ariadne's was, dropping rubbish into a bin
that was brown, and plastic.

Ariadne turned back to face him. 'I don't know what
you want me to do, but I can promise you I won't change
anything else in this house and I will never mention
Marina's name to you again. Is that enough?'

'Enough,' he repeated. She was crying again, reached
for the kitchen towel. 'The bin's new.'

'Oh, Bill, I haven't understood, I haven't understood
at all. I just . . . Please, please, let's start again.' Her mel-
lifluous voice wrapped itself round him. 'I've been trying
to bring some of the brightness of outside into the
inside. You seem to like being out of doors so much better than being inside the house.'

'Indoors is not the same as outside. I've told you
already. It is not the same at all.'

'No.' She walked up and put her arms round him,
rested her head, which reached just to his chin, on his
shoulder. The feel of her against his chest was warm and
comforting.

*

Ariadne fetched the rug from the loft and replaced it in the hall where it was a constant reminder, not of the time when everything was in its place as it had always been, but of the changes that had come upon him. And of Ariadne's falsehoods.

Marina told him that the name Ariadne was derived from the Greek for spider.

'She's wrapping you up in her web, Bill,' she said. 'Watch out she doesn't eat you.' Marina had stopped coming to the house and Ariadne had stopped mentioning her name.

Marina said: 'I'm afraid she doesn't like my friendship with you.'

Ariadne said: 'I think she's trying to turn you against me.'

'That's ridiculous,' he said.

Words had never played much part in their relationship, but even the little conversation they had exchanged had dwindled. Her manner towards him changed from loving to something he could not define. He might almost have thought she was frightened of him, but that was ridiculous. Mindful of Marina's warnings, he was perpetually fearful. Early in his career, he had converted a bedroom into a darkroom; over the years it had developed into an editing suite and an office, where he manipulated photographs and carried out his administration. Now it became his haven. When he was not up Machu Picchu or in the Amazon rainforest, or next door at Mrs Carmichael's, he was in the room at the end of the back corridor, where he felt safe.

There was unrest in Thailand and he came home early. He turned his key in the lock and took a step into the hall, where the faded darkness of the old rug stood firm against the limpid colour of the walls. Then he stopped. Gradually, as he had spoken less and less to Ariadne, she, too, had fallen silent and the house was now as still as it had been in the time after his mother's death. But as he stood in the hall it was filled with a sound he could not remember ever hearing within its walls. So unexpected was it that he first searched his memory for the name of a bird which might make such a noise. But it was not a bird; it was Ariadne, laughing.

He walked through to the kitchen and she was sitting in the sunlight with two children who were giggling in harmony with Ariadne's full-throated laugh. At the sight of him, it all stopped. The children put down their plastic beakers of squash.

'Better go now, Miss,' they said, and scuttled out of the back door.

'You were having fun,' said Bill.

'Yes. It was nothing. Childish things.'

'I don't remember seeing children in the house before.'

'I help out in the school. Those two came to give me a message from the head.'

There was an envelope beside her on the table and Bill

could not rid himself of the feeling that all of this – the children, the beakers, the envelope – was a *trompe l'œil*. If he blinked and refocused, he would see something much more sinister.

'You behave towards me as if I'm a stranger,' Ariadne said, watching him. 'But I'm your wife, Bill. I'm your wife.'

When he was a child his mother used to shut him in the cellar to pay him back for annoying her. Each time, although he knew she would finally let him out, it had felt permanent; a life sentence of darkness and solitude. Ariadne's words were like the cellar door banging shut and the scrape of the key in the lock.

He was carrying the rubbish round from the back of Mrs Carmichael's when Marina suggested he gave her a key to his house.

'I would worry about you less if I knew I could come in and help if there was . . . well, any need to.'

'I can't think why there would be.'

'No, but still. Peace of mind, you know.'

He went that afternoon and had a duplicate cut for the back door.

'I assume you've told her she must stop remodelling your house to suit herself,' Marina said, when he gave it to her.

'I have.'

'I expect all the misunderstanding is behind you now,

then, and you can be happy together. I so much want you to be happy, Bill.'

'I thought you said she was like a spider. You said she wouldn't rest until she had me all trussed up, or something. I forget exactly what you said but it was something like that.'

Marina looked concerned. 'I did say that, but I was hoping you'd forgotten. And I was hoping it wasn't true. You need to give your marriage a chance.'

The advice came too late. The clanging of the cellar door was forever echoing in Bill's mind. When he looked at the objects in his home that had remained the same, it was with the uneasiness of a becalmed sailor who cannot enjoy the respite from a storm for the expectation of the next gale coming. When his eye fell on the unfamiliar, it was with the suspicion of a code-breaker reading an apparently innocent message which he knows might conceal a deadly meaning in its disposition of letters and symbols.

Bill noticed the items on the dresser in the kitchen had been rearranged. Objects had always had their place, and Ariadne, for all her ardour with the paintbrush and her cavalier attitude towards the perfectly serviceable furnishings his mother had chosen, had never disrupted this. The toaster stood to the left of the kettle; Bill's coat hung on the right-hand peg in the hall, Ariadne's (as his mother's had) on the left. The mugs were on the top shelf of the wall cupboard next to the hob, the plates were on the shelf below. The incident with the dresser might, after all, have been carelessness, inattention to the way things ought to be. Ariadne, who was a good housewife, might have inadvertently replaced the toast rack, the eggcups and the pot full of pens in the wrong places after dusting. So Bill did not mention it, just restored them to their correct positions.

When he could not find his gloves in the drawer where gloves were kept, he became angry. Ariadne claimed not to know, any more than he did, where his gloves were, and when they were found on a shelf that was only ever used for hats and scarves, she maintained he must have put them there himself. He put his gloves on his hands and left the house. He walked up to the cliffs and tried to feel that glory in the rightness of the natural world – the patterns and rhythms evolved over millennia – that had delighted him since childhood. He came across an Arctic tern, dead, by the side of the path, from disease or old age, starvation or exhaustion. It lay with its breast uppermost and its wings spread out uselessly by its sides. He recalled the picture Ariadne had made the first time he saw her, cloaked arms held wide as if they were wings ready to lift her off from the sea wall. He walked on. In his work he was used to death and decay; it was a natural part of the natural world and even a part of its beauty. But the image of the tern's limpness in death lingered in his mind.

Walking back to the house, he saw Marina hanging out some washing in Mrs Carmichael's garden. She, too, looked like part of the natural world. A creature of reliable, foreseeable, immutable properties. He stopped at the gate and she walked up to him and laid her palm on his cheek.

'Tell me,' she said. When he had told her, she said: 'You have to be strong. And you have to be vigilant.'

All his life, Bill had watched the natural world with intensity and patience. He had remained motionless, studying plants and wildlife until he understood the fixed and variable patterns of their lives. Indoors, he had noticed nothing. Until Ariadne came, he would have been unable to name the colours or the materials of the decoration and furnishing. He would notice a lack, but could not describe a presence. In the days after his talk with Marina, he looked at the inside of his house in the same way he looked at nature. He studied and committed to memory the details of the disposition of things. He was alert for change, however small, and so close was his observation that he was unnerved by the absence of a layer of dust which he had noted on the sideboard the day before. His feeling of unease grew ever more intense. Because he had never observed so closely before, he did not know whether what struck him for the first time – an arrangement of cushions, the ordering of the books in the bookcase – was as it had been the previous week or not.

He stood at the bedroom window watching Marina pruning roses in Mrs Carmichael's garden. She looked up and raised a hand to him. Ariadne was out; she had gone to her work as a classroom assistant at the primary school. Bill raised his hand in acknowledgement, then beckoned.

Marina walked round the house with him. He had wanted reassurance, but Marina, on crossing the threshold, became a partner in his discomfort.

'I don't know,' she said. 'I can't say what it is, but . . .'

She looked under the chairs, the beds. Opened all the cupboards.

In the bathroom, she turned to him, decisive. 'What you have to do,' she said, 'is wait and watch. You can fix all this . . .' – taking in with the sweep of her arms the precise placement of the towels, the shampoo bottle and the open wall unit where paracetamol, soap and spare toiletries were stacked – 'fix it in your mind and then you'll know when she makes a move. She's trying to unsettle you, Bill, I know she is. She wants to have power over you, or that's the only thing I can imagine, and she's set about achieving it by destroying your comfort and now by messing with your mind. Your mother would have known what to do. Remember that.' She closed the cabinet door and squeezed his arm. 'If ever you need me, just signal. Hang a towel out of the bathroom window and I'll come.'

For the first time in his life, he took photos inside the

house, recording what should have needed no such record.

It was spring and the sun, just rising, edged the early-morning mist with pink. Bill lay awake watching the light growing stronger. He was due to leave, later in the day, for Cambodia, to shoot the pictures for a book on birds of the Far East. He had turned down several contracts in recent months, uneasy in Ariadne's presence but fearful of turning his back on her. This job had been arranged some while ago and there was no avoiding it, so this morning was his last chance to take hold of his fears.

He slipped out of the bed and tiptoed to the bathroom. He smothered his face in shaving foam and picked up his cut-throat razor, to avoid waking Ariadne with the sound of the electric shaver. He drew the blade down the left-hand side of his face, wiping away the soap. The blade was a little blunt, and he opened the door to the wall unit, looking for a safety razor. The tidy stacks of soaps, pills and other things on the left-hand side of the cupboard were undisturbed. But on the right-hand shelf, in front of the boxes of tissues and bottles of shampoo, was a yellow plastic duck. It was set at an angle that made its eye of black paint appear to be looking sideways at him, its bill curved up in a sneer. It was an abomination. This anthropomorphic, reductionist rendering of the beauty and complexity of a wild bird was an insult, and its presence on the shelf – in the house – was an outrage. He could not have missed it when he had stood here with Marina a few days before. He could check that. He had evidence.

Still holding the razor, he walked from the bathroom to his den, and pressed the button on the tablet he had used to fix the elusive contents of his house in the way he knew best. The screen lit up and showed him an image as shocking in its way as the plastic duck in the cupboard. This, too, was a duck; a real duck he had photo-graphed on a mere the last time he had taken the tablet with him on a walk. The pictures of the inside of the house were gone, as if they had never been taken.

Bill's mind, sliding out of control across the tilting surface of his world, came to rest against the strong, sure figure of his mother. He imagined her, walking firmly, her back towards him, leading Boo into the shed. He picked up the razor and, shaving foam still covering half his face, went back into the bedroom.

III

ARIADNE'S STORY

I have spent my life living with people who wanted me there for a purpose. A purpose I have often imperfectly fulfilled. I was adopted, as a baby, by a couple in Coventry. They lived in a perfect house, perfectly maintained. They believed in their own perfection in every respect – their values, their opinions, their personalities, talents, choice of house, furnishings, holidays, clothes . . . Almost every sentence they spoke began with the phrase 'of course'. Adopting children was, so they said, in their childlessness, a right and moral choice. They were able to keep up an air of superiority in the presence of the majority who had made the selfish, messy, planet-cluttering decision to procreate in the normal way. Of course, there was no question but that a child chosen by them would turn out to be perfect. Only, as luck would have it (bad luck, theirs and mine), I did not. It was almost impossible for my mother to claim I was better than the other children in her social circle in any respect.

I was plain, overweight, uninteresting, academically mainstream. The only area in which I excelled, and this was truly my mother's achievement, was behaviour. I was well mannered, quiet, obedient. I was 'no trouble at all'. I behaved as they wanted me to behave. I was to make the same mistake again.

Strange as it seems to me now, I made no effort to escape after school or university, but returned home and did temporary jobs while my mother looked around for someone to marry me. Her plans for the wedding and her starring role as mother of the bride were in place; only the groom was missing. When, after a couple of years, her designs continued to be frustrated by my determined (her word) refusal to make myself pleasant, I decided to take my future into my own hands and began to train as a teacher. In the summer of that year, I went with a group of students from my course to a large, rented house on the west coast. We were a disparate bunch but by the end of the first week coalitions had been formed; twos and threes had clumped together and I found myself solitary. I walked alone along the sea-front, watching the birds rising and falling over the waves. A man came up to me and named the birds. He was a tall, strong, good-looking man and he spoke to me as if he knew who I was; it was as if we were continuing a conversation already started. His words and his manner were not moulded by any social awareness; he wanted to talk to me about birds, and he did. I knew nothing about birds and would normally have attempted to disguise this. Instead, I said: 'I come from Coventry. We don't have many gulls in Coventry.'

'I live just over there,' he said. 'Would you like a cup of tea?'

His name was Bill Flood and he was a wildlife photographer. He seemed to find something in me of which he approved and we embarked on a courtship. It was an odd sort of courtship. He said very little; it had been my habit to say very little, too. The words I spoke in company tended to echo in my own ears after I had spoken them. They bounced back to obliterate the sense of what other people said to me in their turn, so I found it easier not to speak. But Bill needed me to talk; even better, he appeared indifferent to what I spoke about. It was an unexpected pleasure: I could say anything at all, knowing no one would judge it. Now I can see that my uneasiness over what other people thought about what I said is a commonplace agony of youth. But at the time, it seemed an affliction personal to me and I thought I had found an effective salve.

We were married three months after we met. Quietly. I considered inviting my parents, because I wanted to show them that, after all, I was achieving something. I was marrying a man of undeniable good looks, with a healthy income and an international reputation in his field. I realized in time that the news would not have made them think better of me, but only of themselves.

'Of course,' they would have said to each other, 'we are the sort of people whose daughter marries a famous photographer, and that is a credit to us and as it should be.' So I did not invite them or indeed tell them of the step I was taking.

I moved into the seafront house where Bill had lived with his recently deceased mother and set about filling the gap she had left. I didn't think like that at the time; I was convinced we were together because I was in love with him and he with me. I tried to believe I was living happily ever after, but my marriage was too like a fairy tale to be believable. The house was heavy with velvet and polished wood and when Bill went away, as he often did, I sometimes stood by the window looking out at the activity on the front as if I were watching a film. I was a visitor in my own life, even when Bill came home. He was so silent, and though he demonstrated affection by wanting to be wherever I was, in wanting me to talk to him, no matter on what subject, it was all, so to speak, at arm's length. Even literally at arm's length. He did not seek or respond well to physical contact. From the beginning, we made love no more than once a week, and it felt like something Bill needed rather than wanted to do.

I began to focus on the house itself, which I loved. It was orderly, and this was an environment I was used to. It was also my house, the first time I had experienced this, and I surprised myself by having a clear vision of how I wanted it to be: the colour scheme, the type of furniture, the arrangement of ornaments. It was not a vision of radical change and I did not want to upset Bill by imposing it all at once. I discussed each move with him, if our conversations could be called discussion. I said, for example: 'The curtains in the lounge are faded. I thought I might make new ones. Maybe we could have a paler colour.'

He replied: 'They're good, thick curtains. They keep the light out.'

'I'll make sure the new curtains are thick enough to keep the light out.'

This was the way we approached agreements. I made a statement, he made a related statement and I qualified my first position to take into account the opinion he had expressed. Questions, I had discovered, disconcerted him. He did not always respond when I spoke, but, in the beginning, I was careful to take no steps until I was sure he had understood what I intended to do.

At this time, when we had been married about a year and the refurbishment of the house was beginning to take shape, I made a friend. Her name was Marina Blake and she had been at school with Bill, she told me the first time I met her. Now she was a nurse, working shifts at the cottage hospital, and had moved in with an elderly lady called Mrs Carmichael who had the house next door to ours. Marina was a spiky sort of woman; everything about her was wiry – her hair and her body and her limbs. It would have been quite easy to make a passable imitation of her with a few pipe cleaners and strands of wire wool. (And in time it did occur to me to do this.) She had a rather high voice and a habit of standing too close. She was either a sympathetic listener, or intrusive; I could not decide. She said very little about herself but she excavated the person she was talking to, mining them for emotions, information, opinions. It meant that after every meeting with her, I was conscious of having talked too much about myself, and, though she applauded whatever I said, it made me feel uncomfortable. But I was bereft of intimacy. I knew other people in the town, in my role as Bill's wife, and had a few female acquaintances – Fiona, the librarian; Charlotte, the deputy head at the primary school – but I assumed their friendliness towards me was based on a respect for Bill, and I discounted it. I accepted the friendship of Marina Blake.

Marina was as excited as I was about the changes to the house, and she was prepared to be bolder than I would have been, to go further in throwing out the old and introducing the new. She had known Bill all his life, and she engaged with him in a way I could not. While he liked to hear me talking, he seemed to listen to her. So when she claimed knowledge of his likes and dislikes – suggested I remove a rug and a painting and a mirror because, she said, she knew he hated them – I believed her. I wanted to believe her, of course, because I was having fun. And having her approval made me less alert to the way Bill reacted; it was easy to assume he did not mind because he was a man who displayed so little emotion. I still told him beforehand of every change, but I cannot say he had agreed; he had merely said nothing expressive of disagreement. Had I been as anxious to please him as I had been in the beginning, I might have noticed he was becoming uneasy, and slowed the pace of change. Or maybe there was never a moment when I could have made a difference to the outcome, from the day Marina Blake moved in next door.

Bill did challenge a few of the changes I made – objecting to colours I had chosen or household objects I had replaced. I deferred to Marina's greater familiarity with my husband to check if I was going too far, too fast.

'No, no,' she said. 'It's good he's taking notice. He needs to be pulled out of himself, made to sit up and pay attention.'

Despite her reassurance, I was worried about our relationship; mine and Bill's. I began to feel I was fulfilling the role of wife (or mother substitute) less adequately than Marina would have done. When he was home, he was so often next door, doing what Marina called 'little jobs' for her. When he was away, she was constantly in my house, giving advice, poking about. It began to feel as if she thought she had a better right to be there than I did. She walked in without ringing the bell; she picked up letters from the hallway and turned them over, speculating on the contents; I would leave her in one room while I went to make tea or put something away and when I came back she had taken herself off to another part of the house, opening drawers, looking in cupboards. She never showed any consciousness that this was behaviour that might be resented and although I did resent it, I was not capable of telling her so. I realize now that this was not normal behaviour, on her part or on mine. She had a lack of boundaries that would have been intolerable to most people, but most people had not experienced my upbringing. I had been trained to believe that, if I disagreed with those around me, I was certainly wrong. I had avoided conflict all my life and did not have the skills to deal with it. I allowed Marina to infiltrate my marriage, although even as I yielded to her influence, I was beginning to mistrust her.

Bill came home unexpectedly, although he told me he had left a message. If he had, and he lacked the imagination to lie, it had been deleted before I listened to it. He commented at once on something I had, with Marina's encouragement, changed in the house. I told him it was Marina's idea. I had said this before, when he had made similar comments, and assumed he had believed me; I had taken his lack of response for acceptance. I should have known better. This time, he said:

'That's a lie.'

'How do you know?'

'Marina has told me the truth.'

It was like the moment when you step out on to what you believe is level ground and find you have overlooked a step and are, all of a sudden, off balance, certain to fall, but how far and with what impact is momentarily uncertain. I had thought, when I was first married, that there would be no bliss greater than being loved by a handsome and successful man, having a home of my own. But even at its best, it was an agonizing bliss. I had felt breathless from the wonder of it and the fear of losing it. And now I knew I had lost it. I was overwhelmed with a realization of my own powerlessness. Marina knew him so well; if she chose to manipulate me and my husband to drive us apart, I knew I could not resist. I began to cry, something Bill hated, but even as I was sobbing into a wet tissue, I had given up hope of going into battle against her. Just as I had accepted my role as the unsatisfactory daughter, I resigned myself to being the unsatisfactory wife. Of course, I stopped speaking to Marina; I locked the doors to keep her out, dropped any pretence of friendship. But I could do nothing to justify myself to my husband; I did not even try.

I had hoped for children from my marriage, but when that had not happened after a year and a half, I went out to look for a job with the children of others. Charlotte took me on as a classroom assistant at the primary school. If I am mapping the contours, the heights and the depths of my life, those hours with six- and seven-year-olds were as far above sea level as it got. In the weeks after the realization of Marina's treachery, I began to work more hours at the school, on a voluntary basis, because it was the only time I was happy, the only time I felt safe. Inside the house, I began to be afraid. I was afraid of Marina. Even when I had not seen her for days, I could sense her malevolent presence. And I began to worry about my own sanity. Bill was becoming more and more remote, speaking less, withdrawing even those few gestures of affection he used to make. His exchanges with me were all about the misplacing of objects. It was an orderly house, as I have said, when I moved in, and I like order so I had kept up the tradition of everything having a place. Now things were, repeatedly, not in their place and I could not remember having moved them. I was at a loss to explain why this was happening, and each of the explanations that occurred to me was frightening. I thought I might be sleepwalking or having blackouts and did not know what I was doing; or that Bill was moving them and pretending he had not; or that Marina was still coming into my house, through locked doors, when I was not at home; or that Marina's evil spirit had penetrated the walls and become, like a poltergeist, a moving force within them. I was terrified of the implications of any of these, and I was particularly terrified of Marina Blake. I was not frightened of Bill, though, which just shows how little I had understood, because he tried to kill me.

I can only describe what happened on that morning by what others have told me since. My own memory is restricted to a moment of terrifying pain and then a sense of being elsewhere. I have no memory of a last glimpse of Bill's face; he drew the razor across my throat as I slept. I do not remember Marina being in the room, although she was there. She came into the house using a key Bill must have given her and found me bleeding to death. She called the ambulance first and then the police and only when they came did they find Bill's body, hanging from the pipes in the basement, a twisted sheet still covered in my blood round his neck.

Bill Flood was not an easy man to love and I know now that what I felt for him in the early days of our marriage was not love but an obsessive form of gratitude. Marina Blake has told me since he died that she loved him, but this is equally untrue. She felt she owned him.

She saved my life. There can be no doubt of that. She was, after all, a nurse and knew where to apply pressure, what were the right actions to take, so I made it to the hospital. I had never encountered violence before; I had never been in hospital, had hardly been ill. It may be hard to believe, but being a patient was more unsettling, more disconcerting for me than the actual incident. I was completely adrift, unable even to cry out in lamentation or in an appeal for help because my vocal cords had been damaged in the attack. I had no one to turn to. My parents did not even know my married name. I had had no gift for forming friendships and had kept up with no one from school or college. I had made no close friends locally, except Marina. So, remarkable as it may appear, I was pleased to see her when I woke up. She was in and out all the time, travelling some distance to the hospital where I was first admitted and then, when I was moved to the local hospital where she worked, she was the only thread that linked me to the world I had so nearly left.

At first I felt unwilling to live. I thought I would not survive this and, on the whole, I preferred the idea that I would not, that I need no longer endure it. Then I became aware that I had survived and, despite myself, would survive, and this was the more terrifying realization, because how on earth would I be able to carry on the business of living when I had no power of any kind? I could, I realized later, have reached out to any of the well-wishers around my bed – the chaplain, the counsellor, the few people from the town who visited and who, as later events proved, had more goodwill towards me than I imagined I justified. But it did not occur to me that any of these comparative strangers would do anything except shake their heads and look puzzled if, through gestures and the written word, I had sought their help. Even if I had, they would almost certainly have been taken in by Marina's assertion of her right to care for me, and would have let events follow the same course. From the moment I entered the hospital alive, I was doomed to leave it as a prisoner of Marina's apparent altruism. It did not alter the outcome that I knew it was her ill will and cunning that had driven Bill to do what he did. I still clung to her when she appeared at my bedside. But I think it did enhance my helplessness subsequently, convinced me I was too pathetic to act on my own behalf.

She took me home to my own house and installed me in my own bedroom and kept me there, almost without effort. Just a little planning and anticipation were all that was required for me to become an invisible, voiceless object of pity. She was very clever about it. I realized that over the months as I began to reach out and found how close about me the walls had been built. She began to work permanent night shifts, which meant she was always in the house when I was awake, and I was not truly awake for much of the time. I took pills, kept by Marina, prescribed by a doctor Marina took me to see who only had her word for it how I was feeling, and who discussed the drugs I should be taking with her by name rather than by effect, so I had no idea what they were.

Whether Marina was in the house or out of it, the doors were locked. They needed an old-fashioned key to open them, and I had no keys. I also had no money and no cards. No handbag. No mobile phone. There were two computers in the house, a laptop and a desktop, but they were in Bill's study, which was locked. The only way of communicating with the outside world from inside the house was with a landline. No use at all to someone who could not speak. It took eight or nine months to find all this out, which would seem absurdly long to an ordinary, healthy person. Once I had finally grasped my lack of basic tools for living, I noticed something else. Looking round for some way of confronting Marina, I realized there was no blank paper and nothing to write with anywhere that I could reach.

Marina's manner towards me, during the months I spent finding out how total her control was, how completely I was at her mercy, was kind and condescending. I was able to believe that she had not meant to put me in this position, so the next time she started scrolling through texts on her phone, I put my hand on it and pointed at myself.

'What?' she said, looking up. I repeated the gesture, and she laughed. 'Don't be ridiculous, Ariadne, what use would you have for a mobile phone?' I made a texting movement with my thumbs. 'Oh, really? And who are you going to send texts to? You have friends and relations, do you?' I pointed at her. 'Well now,' she said, leaning towards me, 'you never need to text me because you have nothing to tell me I don't already know. I know exactly where you are every hour of the day, and unless

I'm with you, it's inside this house. Don't think it's going to be easy to escape now you think you're better. You destroyed my life when you married Bill and you are going to have to pay for it.'

I was shocked and frightened and began to cry; she reverted at once to her usual manner, soothing me as an adult would a child. This became a feature of our life together; I would, through grunts and gestures, express frustration and she would respond by reminding me how much she had lost, how large was the debt I owed and the extent to which I was helpless. Then she would be soothing and playful, as if we were close, albeit unequal, partners in life. I still do not know what was the purpose I served in being her prisoner: whether, as she said, she was exacting revenge, or whether she was buying respect in the town for her selflessness, or whether she just could not resist the pleasure of having complete power over another person. It hardly mattered. I was her plaything, and she became an increasingly cruel playmate. When I irritated her, or her mood was soured by some circumstance I knew nothing of, she began to add physical to verbal abuse. Nothing of consequence, just a shove, a tug on my hair, a pinch on the arm. Enough to remind me how vulnerable I was.

I did see other people. We went out, together, of course, to the supermarket and the library, to the cinema. Marina, naturally, spoke for me on these occasions, interposed herself between me and whoever came forward to speak to us. I preferred this; I did not want to be noticed. I looked hideous, and not just because of the grotesque scar around my neck but because Marina had control of all aspects of my appearance. Although I had never been proud of the way I looked, I had a certain style and felt I presented myself in a way which, at the least, did not accentuate my disadvantages. Now I was forced to go out with my hair hanging limply round my face, without make-up, and wearing dresses in vile colours and materials, little better than smocks. I had no tights, only pop socks, and the hems of the dresses were not long enough to hide the tops of these. So even though I longed to escape, I also did not wish to go out. I looked, I knew, like someone without a good enough grip on things to make herself presentable. I looked as if my problems were mental as well as physical. Most of the town, I subsequently found out, believed this to be the case. My inability to tell any of the people I met of what was happening to me was not, therefore, entirely down to my loss of the power of speech. Whatever I said, as it were, about wanting to escape from Marina would be discounted as a disorder of the mind, understandable in the circumstances.

Apart from Bill's study, I could go anywhere in the house, and I found myself again, as I had at the beginning of my marriage, standing in the front room looking out at the seafront, watching people passing, the gulls rising and diving. I watched as the seasons changed and the sparkle of the sun on the sea gave way to high tides and high winds lifting the waves to break over the railings; as the frost lying thickly in the shadow of the benches melted and the spring bedding plants in the municipal planters began to unfold their orange, pink and purple petals. For well over a year I did nothing to free myself. I let it happen as I had let my parents subdue and belittle me, and as I had let Marina tell Bill stories about me. I hated myself almost as much as I hated Marina. I thought about suicide, but hopelessly, sure I would never have the courage to go through with it. I thought about taking a kitchen knife – she was not careful with those – and stabbing Marina, but my only experience of violence had rendered me forever incapable of inflicting it. I could, I convinced myself, do nothing except endure it. And I did. Until – how to describe it? – I had the strangest moment.

Marina had her reading group in the house; she was not much of a reader but liked being part of the group. I was upstairs in my room, but remembered, early in the evening, that I had left the book I was reading – and reading was almost my only pleasure – in the kitchen, so I went down the back stairs to retrieve it, not wanting to risk meeting anyone in the hallway. When I reached the kitchen there was a woman standing looking at me. I had never seen her before. Strangers in the street tried to pretend they had not seen me, but she looked straight at me, with apparent interest. The idea came into my head that maybe I could tell a total stranger what was going on more easily than I could speak to people I knew. I believe I made some sort of noise, as if I had, for a second, forgotten I could not pour it all out to her. Then Marina came in and led me away. In that moment, though, I had finally understood that I had only myself to blame. It was up to me to take action, on my own behalf, and, whatever the consequences, I would do so.

The first thing I had to do was to stop swallowing the pills. I knew there were sleeping pills and anti-depressants among them; I was asleep for all of the night and much of the day and felt disorientated and listless when I was awake. I was properly awake for just a few hours in the afternoon when, whether she was working that night or not, Marina was sure to be with me. I needed time alone, and a clear head, to have any chance of helping myself.

I did not know which pills were which, and it was beyond me to manipulate into my sleeve or hold in my cheek all dozen of them, so I experimented. By cutting out first one, then another, I was able to identify the anti-depressants and the sleeping pills. Failing to take these made me anxious, slightly dizzy and unable to sleep. But I persevered, spitting them out when Marina's back was turned. I embraced the discomfort as evidence that I was making an effort, suffering in the cause of freedom. It felt like my first triumph, overcoming the side effects. And gradually, it worked. I began to feel alert, and ready to take the next steps. Now I could stay awake after Marina had gone, I could prowl around the house at will, but this only confirmed what my previous wanderings, in a drugged state, had shown me. There was nothing to find to help me escape: no spare keys, no means of communication. For this, I had to access Bill's study.

Marina used a red handbag of soft leather, the shape and texture suggestive of a giant tomato on the point of going rotten. (Of all the things I hated about Marina, not the least was the jarring note she struck against the colours and shapes I had chosen for the house I wanted to live in.) Had she felt less contempt for me than she did, she would have kept this bag, or at least the keys in it, somewhere out of my reach, but she didn't. She left it on the hall table. I formulated a plan. In the dead of night, when she was out at work, I practised moving about without making a sound. I went down the stairs from my bedroom to the hall, up the stairs from the hall to the study, down the stairs from the study to the hall, up the stairs from the hall to my bedroom. At first I concentrated on controlling my movements, which had become heavy and clumsy during more than a year and a half almost entirely indoors. When I had learned to step lightly again, from foot to foot, I began to memorize the route, eliminate the possibility of a misstep or a stumble.

Bedroom door to first stair: five steps, left hand on to

newel post, twelve treads down to the hall, four steps to
the hall table, four steps back, right hand on the newel
post, twelve treads to the landing, eight steps along the
corridor to the study door, eight steps back, left hand on
newel post, twelve treads down, four steps to table, four
steps back, right hand on newel post, twelve treads up,
five steps to bedroom door. There were loose boards on
the second and fourth treads from the top; a curl in the
edge of the rug on the corridor to the study which could
trip me up; the coats hanging on the wall at the bottom
of the stairs could catch my shoulder and a belt buckle
might strike the mirror as they settled back in their
places. I mapped these hazards in my mind as I travelled
down, and as I travelled back. I fell into a routine. Five,
newel post, keep left, twelve, newel post, keep left, four.
Four, keep right, newel post, keep right, twelve, newel
post, keep left, eight. Keep right, eight, newel post, keep
left, twelve, newel post, keep left, four. Four, keep right,
newel post, keep right, twelve, newel post, five. At last I
was ready, and while Marina slept during the day, I went
downstairs, removed her keys from the bag, went back
to the study door. Now I had to do something I had not
been able to practise – turn the key in the lock. I listened
for sounds from her bedroom on the floor above. There
were none. The key went in smoothly; the lock turned
without a sound. By the time she woke up, her keys were
back in the bag and I was in bed. If she tried the study
door before I had a chance to lock it again, she would

almost certainly assume she had forgotten to turn the key the last time she left. She would never imagine I was capable of having done it.

She did not try the door that day, and when she had gone to work I was able to enter Bill's study for the first time since his death. Beneath the dust and the stale air, it still held the distinctive odour from the days when Bill worked in there, when I sat on the other side of the desk doing accounts on the desktop computer while he manipulated images on the laptop. For a moment, I was overwhelmed with sorrow for the lost promise of our first year together, but the menace of Marina, miles away as she was, was more powerful than the memory of my husband, and I wanted to be gone from there as soon as I could. I checked the laptop first, but she had changed the password and I could not open it. She had not touched the PC, though. The password had not been changed and the last security scan had been on the day before Bill died. I had an e-mail account I could access through that machine. It was available to me, as I sat there, close to midnight, alone in the house. I could use it to tell someone outside the house what was happening to me. But who? And what would that lead to? They would e-mail back, perhaps, in the morning, when they had read what I had written, and I would not reply, because by then I would be locked out of the room. They would come round – say it was the police I had e-mailed, or Fiona, or Charlotte – to see if I was all right, and Marina would spin her web round them. And then – I could hardly bear the thought – she would find out I had made the attempt to escape. I had no idea what she was capable of, in the circumstances. I shut the machine down.

The desk was locked but there were papers in a tray, and the one on top was a bank statement. It was for an account I had held before Bill died, in my own name, and it showed significant sums of money had been paid in, during the last month, and then withdrawn. They went in from various sources – I could not work out where – and went out again to 'client account'. I could have learned more online, but for that I needed a debit card and a security device, and I had neither. The statement did clear up one other mystery, though. No post was delivered to my house and when I looked at the address for the account – my account – it was next door. Mrs Carmichael's house, where Marina used to live; now empty, because the old lady had moved into a nursing home.

By now I was beginning to shake; it was cold and at the back of my mind was the awful, fuzzy, sticklike outline of Marina appearing in the doorway, come home early for some reason, creeping up the stairs as I had crept down them the day before. I had no idea what she would do, but I could imagine violence, and my flesh cringed from it. My hands were unsteady as I straightened the pile of papers, checked the positioning of the laptop and the mouse, shut the door behind me.

Next day, I waited for Marina to go to sleep, then set off on my journey. Five newel post keep left twelve newel post keep left four. Now I had the keys in my hand. Four keep right newel post keep right twelve newel post keep left eight. The study door was locked. Keep right eight newel post keep left twelve keep left four. The keys were back in her bag. Four keep right newel post keep right twelve . . . I had not given myself enough time, in the last few days and nights, to sleep. I was weary and tense and I stumbled. Marina was at once on the landing.

'What are you doing? Why aren't you in bed?'

I sat down on the top step and moaned, shaking my head from side to side, as if I was unhappy and confused, as indeed I had been for so long.

'Back to your room,' she said. 'You're such a trial.'

I lay in bed, gripping the edge of the sheet, terrified yet triumphant.

After this came Marina's nights off and I was not alone in the house for four days. During this time, I thought about what I had achieved and what I should do next. There must be, I reasoned, another set of keys, for Bill and I had each had a set. I had looked everywhere; the only place left was the locked desk in Bill's study.

Meanwhile, I met, for the second time, the woman

from that night in the kitchen. She was in the library, talking to Fiona, the librarian. Fiona was, of all the women I had known in former times, the one who managed to come closest to treating me now as she had then. She selected books I might like to read and talked to me about them as if she believed I had as good a brain, and as sharp a judgement, as she did. She told me that the stranger – her name, curiously, was Hope, which I took as a good omen, though I never found out if this was her first or last name – was a writer organizing events in the town, and one of these was to be a writing competition, on the theme of 'Memory'. She offered me an entry form and I put out my hand for it but Marina was, in the instant, at my side, taking it away, whispering about my supposedly precarious mental state. I watched Fiona and Hope watching me and the feeling of resurgent power such as I had felt in the kitchen, the sudden rush of energy a man might feel as he realizes he is at risk of drowning, came to me again. Marina bent down to put the books I had chosen in a bag; I made eye contact with Fiona and nodded.

Marina went back to work and I stole her keys again when she was asleep in the morning: five newel post keep left twelve newel post keep left four, keys in my hand. Four keep right newel post keep right twelve newel post keep left eight door unlocked. Only this time, I opened the door and unlocked the desk. I could hear Marina snoring; I almost convinced myself I was not frightened. Keep right eight newel post keep left twelve newel post keep left four. Keys back in the bag. Four keep right newel post keep right twelve newel post five. I was back in bed. It was done. The door and the desk were at my disposal when she went to work that night. I started with the bottom drawer and there, right at the back, was a complete set of keys. I made a noise which, in a person with undamaged vocal cords, might have been a whoop, but which came out as a growl. I looked round at once, as if even this slight noise might have been heard by Marina, far away as she was. Then I held the keys in both hands, savouring the moment. I was free; I had access to everything in the house, and to the street outside, if ever I had the courage to open the front door. Next, the middle drawer: there was a notebook in which she had written all her passwords, so I had access to the laptop, as well. Finally, the top drawer: I found a power of attorney, signed by me – and it was my signature, albeit shaky, witnessed by a nurse in the hospital where I had first been admitted – giving her complete control of my financial affairs. So I had access to the world outside the house, and to information, but I still had no access to my own money.

I was shaking again, and it took me a long time to satisfy myself that I had left no sign of my visit, no indent in the chair cushion, no stray dark hairs, no disturbance of the surface of the desk. Just a few days before, there had been a small but telling escalation in the violence. She had been reading the local paper at the kitchen table and stood up to put a mug in the sink. I reached across to move the paper so I could read an article on the page she had open. She turned round at the movement and smashed the mug against my knuckles.

'Get off that!' she shouted. 'I haven't finished. Who do you think you are?'

I whimpered, holding my bruised knuckles, keeping my eyes down, my posture cowed, but inwardly formulating an answer to that question: 'You will find out soon enough who I am.'

This incident convinced me that I had to find a hiding place for my set of keys which she would never discover. The house was (thanks to my influence) uncluttered and Marina, I must admit, was a tireless little body when it came to keeping it looking neat, so there were no corners or containers likely to remain undisturbed. But she only ever cooked a limited range of dishes, being uninterested in food, and there were jars in the cupboard left over from the days when I had decided what I would eat. I hid the keys in a storage jar full of lentils. I was quite sure Marina would have no notion what to do with a lentil.

When Marina was there, I was trying to be exactly as I had been: submissive, slow-witted, half asleep, occasionally truculent. With the keys safely hidden in the lentils, it became easier to act like this because, strange as it may seem, this was how I felt. Deeply uncertain. I was too aware of the unanswered and unanswerable questions: what should I do now? What would Marina do in reaction to what I did next? I was, suddenly, in a position of some power. I could undermine her as she had undermined me in the last weeks of Bill's life. I could change the password on the laptop so she could not access it. I could have the locks changed (if I stole money from her purse and wrote down my instructions). I could walk out, vanish; go to Coventry, for example. When I was at school I attended some sessions designed to make us better citizens or some such thing. We were told to work out what success looked like, before putting a plan into action. According to the theory, it was important to imagine yourself in the post-implementation sunlight, able to look around and say, 'Yes, this is how I wanted it to be.' I had no ambitions at the time so it had no application to me, but I remembered it now. What did I want my life to be like, in an ideal world? I did not know if I was capable of living on my own, physically or emotionally. I had never done so. When I started to prowl round the house I was obsessed with hatred for Marina, for her manipulative nature, her nastiness, her jarring presence. But, after all, could I cope without her? If I had money as well as keys, it might be possible to avoid confrontation, she might accept our changed relationship and we could co-exist. Then I remembered the blows she had already inflicted and realized how weak I was; I was imagining a calm and peaceful outcome that was never going to be possible. It was unimaginable that she would leave without being forced, physically, to do so. It was more likely that she would kill me, or, if I survived, I would be permanently damaged; more, even, than I had been by Bill's attack. Having faced this and understood it was the price I might have to pay if I carried on trying to escape, I was calmer, and I made my next visit to Bill's study during the night, to see if I could understand the financial transactions.

Marina was orderly in her management of information on the laptop. There was a file folder called *Finance*, with several sub-folders. I looked in one – *Investments* – which was mainly statements of profit and capital growth on different portfolios. It meant nothing to me. I downloaded the folder on to a memory stick I found in the drawer, and opened her e-mail account. Here, too, there were folders. I opened *Bill's Estate* and began to go through the exchanges of messages. Two things gradually became clear. The first was that Bill had left everything to me – had made a will since our marriage leaving everything to me – which surprised me as we had not spoken of it, though, given the assignments he went on, it was a sensible precaution. The second was that he had been a man of considerable wealth, according to my view of these things. The royalty payments on pictures reprinted in books and periodicals I had been aware of, and knew they represented an income I could live on, but in addition there was accumulated capital, not to mention the value of the house, that looked like riches to me. I downloaded this folder, too, and uploaded both to the desktop, erased them from the stick and returned it to precisely the same position it had been in before.

All this took time; it was late and I was tired by the time I left the room and put the keys back in the jar. This must have made me careless, because next morning, there was a scattering of lentils on the kitchen floor, little orange discs on the oatmeal tiles. If they had been arranged to spell out the word 'DEATH' they could not have terrified me more.

'What's this?' said Marina, kneeling to sweep them up. 'What on earth have you been up to in the night? Or are you going to tell me it was mice?' I shrugged, trying to indicate it was a matter of indifference to me where the lentils had come from. She opened the cupboard beside her and looked inside, then back at the contents of her dustpan. 'Everything is in jars!' she said. 'It can't have been mice. Have you been fiddling in this cupboard?' She reached out a hand to pick up the nearest jar. The lentil jar.

Beside me on the table was the teapot, full of freshly brewed tea. As Marina's hand approached the jar, my hand moved to the teapot, two co-ordinated actions carried out in a second that lasted a lifetime. Before she had lifted the jar from the shelf, the teapot landed on the floor and broke apart, spraying tea over Marina's legs as she crouched by the open cupboard, splashing on to the nurse's uniform she still wore. I started to bellow, as if in pain or frustration, wagging my head from side to side, trying to divert her, at all costs, from the cupboard beside her. She leaped to her feet, grabbed my arm, and hit me. It was a hard blow; I suspect it would have been harder if she had hit her first target, my face, but she changed the direction at the last moment and caught me on the shoulder. I staggered back, only her grip on my arm preventing me from falling, then she let me go, and as I started to crumple, she kicked my legs. I fell to the floor, at eye level with shards of china, a slick of tea and a telltale red lentil. Marina stood over me, breathing heavily. I tensed in expectation of another kick, but she had, it seemed, done enough to satisfy her punitive instincts. She had underestimated me again; she had no suspicion that the lentils and the broken teapot indicated anything more than clumsiness on my part.

'Get this cleaned up,' she said. 'I'm going to bed.'

I snatched the keys out of the lentil jar as soon as her footsteps reached the top landing. This time, I put them in the pocket of my thick winter coat hanging in the hall. By the time winter came, I would be free of her. The blow she had just struck made me certain of that. I would be free, one way or another.

*

The following week we went to the library again and when I opened one of the books Fiona had selected, I found she had slipped in an entry form for the writing competition, and three or four sheets of lined paper. It was the first time anyone had made a gesture implying understanding. Fiona must have understood that Marina had made a choice for me, in respect of the competition, and I had had no power to overturn the decision she had made. It gave me hope.

Over the next few nights I wrote a paragraph for Fiona which was emotional, not factual. The facts were too many and too complicated; the emotions were so strong it was much easier to express them and, I thought, it would at least give Fiona a sense of the despair I felt. I put my e-mail address on the back of the form and walked to the library to put it through the letter-box. I waited until the streets were empty, around midnight, unlocked the front door and went out on to the pavement. It was a fine night, the sea gently murmuring on the other side of the wall, the distant beat of a party being held in a cove round the headland. It was half a mile to the library and I felt every step to be a positive action, an assertion of freedom. I met two young people walking close together, her hand in the back pocket of his jeans, his hand in the back pocket of her jeans, enjoying an adolescence that I had missed entirely. I met a drunk, vomiting into a drain. I might once have felt nervous on these streets, at this time. If someone had attacked me now, I would have been furious at this interruption to my plans, but I had no serious fears that anyone would.

I received an e-mail from Fiona.

'I found your submission quite shocking,' she wrote. 'Do you want to come round for coffee and a chat? (Paper and pencils provided!)'

'I need to explain,' I wrote back, and told her everything I have written here about the level of control Marina was exercising over my life and over my financial affairs. 'I realize it was weak of me to let this happen, but I am determined it cannot go on. Will you help me?'

'I have to ask,' she replied, 'are you sure? This sounds like extreme behaviour and Marina has always seemed to be such a caring person. I am puzzled about what her motive would be. I'm sorry if I sound like a doubting Thomas, but you must admit it is a shocking story and I am having difficulty taking it all in.'

This e-mail was alarming. Even though Fiona's reaction was what I had expected – in fact, she was less sceptical than I had always assumed anyone in the town would be if I shared my side of the story. But there was a risk she would talk to Marina. I e-mailed back.

'It is hard to believe, but it is all true. I know this might seem as if I am being as devious as I claim she is being, but please, please don't confront her with these accusations. I am truly fearful of what she might do.'

Before I could access any reply to this, Charlotte, the deputy head from the primary school, called at the house when Marina was there. This was not unusual. Marina's friends often dropped in. They would be courteous to me, on these occasions, but once the greetings were over, the conversation would go on as if I was not in the room. How would it not, when I could not join in? This time, though, Charlotte told Marina she had come to see me.

'I wonder,' she said, smiling at me, 'if you would like to come to the Year Six concert on Friday afternoon? You'll remember the children from when you helped out, and I thought you might enjoy seeing them again before they escape to secondary school.'

'I'll have to check,' said Marina. 'Let me look at the calendar.' She stood up to take it down from the wall. Charlotte continued to look at me and I nodded, attempted a smile. 'No, I'm sorry,' Marina said, sitting back down, 'my mother has a hospital appointment on Friday afternoon and I need to take her. That's a shame,' and she patted my hand as if regretting having to deny me a treat.

'Well, it's a pity you'll miss it,' said Charlotte. 'But that doesn't stop Ariadne coming, does it?' Turning to me, she said: 'If you don't fancy walking over there on your own, I'll get a member of staff to come and collect you.'

Marina sighed and looked sorrowful. 'I suppose I

could try and rearrange the appointment. If Ariadne really wants to go. You see' – she shifted slightly so her back was half turned towards me and lowered her voice – 'I really don't like to risk letting her go anywhere alone. She is still in a very fragile state.'

'Don't you trust me to look after her, if any looking after is needed?' said Charlotte. She is a fluffy, twittering sort of woman, unlike Fiona, who is tough and forth-right. But she is capable of squaring up to a classroom of children and presenting a solid front, a not-to-be-messed-with manner at odds with her normal, fussy imprecision. She looked at Marina now as if she were that classroom, failing to settle down when told. Before Marina could speak, she looked at me and said, 'I'll send an escort at two o'clock on Friday.'

When she had gone, Marina pinched me. 'Do-gooders,' she said. 'I hate them.'

Later, I heard her phoning the hospital to change her mother's appointment.

I had another e-mail from Fiona.

'I'm beginning to believe you,' she said. 'It seems to me you need to cancel the power of attorney so you can access your own money. I can put you in touch with a solicitor who could do that for you. I also think he should look at the financial transactions, to see what he can make of them.'

I zipped up the files I had downloaded from the

laptop and sent them to the solicitor she named. His name was Edgar, and I remembered having met him, before Bill's death, and being overawed by the height and the hairiness of him.

Just at this time, Marina's mother fell ill. Her father was dead but her mother still lived in a cottage further up the hill. She was a sorry little woman, who never spoke except to express disagreement. I suspect she had a negative or maybe even tormented life, so who can blame her for being sour in old age? It was unthinkable that Marina, with her reputation as the most caring woman in the world, should not step in to look after her, and suddenly I had time during the day to sit at the computer and exchange e-mails with Fiona and with the firm of solicitors, as if I was a woman like any other, a woman with control over her own life. The solicitor asked for a meeting and Fiona offered to go with me. I found some of my old clothes to wear for this occasion, took trouble with my hair, with the disposition of the scarf hiding the scar. We walked to his office – it is a small town – and Fiona greeted people she knew as we passed. Many of them stopped to tell me how pleased they were to see me out, looking well. I was unsettled by this; uncertain how to respond, yet aware of a feeling of well-being I would be able to take out and treasure later, at the kindness of these acquaintances.

I had never spoken to Edgar for more than a few minutes, so it surprised me how warm his greeting was, how much concern he showed for me, before I had even sat down. He took my hand in both of his huge hands, bending his head to look at me with an expression such as a doctor might have, looking for evidence of returning health. I think he was checking how resilient I seemed to be, because, while I thought I had come to sign the paperwork to regain control of my bank account, he had something else to tell me. Marina, he said, was systematically defrauding me. The money going into the account was all mine; the money leaving it was going to accounts she controlled. The investments were slowly being shifted into her name. She was investigating, so the information I had provided indicated, whether it was possible to transfer the ownership of the property. She was robbing me of money, as well as freedom and self-respect, and I was actually heartened by this discovery. Embezzlement is a crime, and the force of the law was much greater than anything I could deploy.

'We have to decide,' said Edgar, 'what you are going to do now. The relevant authorities have been informed but in the meantime, she is still living in your house, and I imagine that is a situation you would like to change. I think I would advise you to ask her to leave before she finds out we have uncovered her fraud.'

Fiona said: 'You could ask her to leave, now, couldn't you?'

I hadn't told Fiona of the lentil incident; I hadn't

mentioned my fear of violence. I was trying to be the sort of woman a woman like Fiona would respect. Now I was forced to confront both how frightened I was and how vindictive I wanted to be. For so long, in the days of crushing misery, I had dreamed of all the ways in which I could expose, humiliate and shame her, but now I had to wonder if I would feel better or worse for indulging myself in this way. I could just change the locks and exclude her (I could imagine with acute pleasure the look of bafflement on her face as she looked up at the house where so much of her malicious energy had been invested, realizing she was locked out of the nest she had so painstakingly feathered for herself). But if things were as anyone seeing our relationship from the outside would assume them to be, this would look petty and mean. I was resolute that I did not want to look petty and mean, so I said I would, as they suggested, ask Marina, politely, to leave. Thank her for what was, by now, more than two years of care and say I no longer needed to put her to the trouble of providing it.

Of course, I could say none of this; I would have to write a letter, which pretended we stood fairly on the ground others believed we stood on, suggesting that she might want to return to living with her mother, or, as I knew she had access, to the house next door.

Fiona touched my hand when this had been decided. 'I think you should have someone with you, when you give it to her,' she said.

'We'll both be there,' said Edgar.

I hugged them both before we left.

We sat at the kitchen table as Marina let herself in.

'Ariadne!' she called, as was usual. As usual, I grunted to indicate where I was.

We heard the rattling of her keys as she locked the door behind her.

'God, I wish that woman would hurry up and die,' she said. 'I'm fed up to the back teeth with her moaning. At least you can't do that.' And she walked into the kitchen, smiling.

It took a moment for her to realize I was not alone, and the upward tilt of her lips, the creases in her cheeks, only faded away slowly as if she had simply forgotten to rearrange her face.

'Hello, Marina,' said Fiona. 'How is your mother?'

'Not good, I'm afraid.' Her eyes were everywhere, taking in the three of us, the paper on the table, the cups of coffee. 'I'm sorry, I'm a bit puzzled as to how you got in. It's not that I'm not pleased to see you, but I always make sure Ariadne is safe by locking the doors. She is my responsibility, you see, and I do worry she might wander off and goodness knows what harm it would do, in her condition, if she met with situations she couldn't handle.'

'What is her condition, exactly?' asked Edgar.

'Well, that's a little hard to sum up, in layman's terms.

But there is the throat trauma, obviously, with its associated neuropathy, and she also suffers from confusion and clinical depression.'

'No, I don't,' I wrote on a piece of paper and pushed it towards her.

She smiled and patted my hand. 'You're so brave, Ariadne. Think positive, good girl. But it is a fact nevertheless.'

I picked up the letter and handed it to her. She took it reluctantly and paused before looking down at it, still moving her eyes around as if she would be able to work out exactly what had happened, how far her power had been eroded, by some clue in the room. She was, I imagine, running through ways to react that might limit the damage, but she was not in possession of enough information to be able to select an approach.

She dropped her eyes and started to read. Not one of us spoke. She sat looking at the paper long after she must have finished reading it, while we waited to find out how she was going to play it. Eventually she looked up, straight at me, with tears in her eyes.

'Is this the thanks I get, Ariadne? Is this the payback for months and months of putting you first, of working nights to be with you during the day, of attending to your every need?' Her voice started to rise. 'I can't believe you could be so ungrateful for everything I've done for you. Where would you have gone, if I hadn't been here for you? How would you have managed the everyday business of living? And after all that, you're simply saying: "Go." I hadn't thought you could be so cruel.' Then she gave herself a shake, wiped the back of her hand across her eyes and stood up. 'I will leave at once, of course.' And she walked out of the room.

I didn't realize I was shaking until Fiona put her arms around me and held me still. What Marina had said was true. She had come to my aid when I needed someone; she had put me first – everything she did was shaped around me. If the others had not been there, who knows if Marina would have had to use violence to induce me to let her stay – for a week, a month, for ever? My ability to resist her, so steady when she was not with me, could be undermined so easily by her distorted truths which I could not help recognizing, nevertheless, as true.

We sat in silence, listening to her moving about upstairs. It was not long before she came back.

'Ariadne, have you taken my laptop?' she asked. 'I'm afraid I need that back. It has private, personal information on it.'

'I have it,' said Edgar. 'It is Ariadne's property, in fact, but if you would care to make an appointment to come into my office, it would be very helpful to go through what is on there together. Ariadne needs to take back control of her financial affairs, as I'm sure you realize, and I'm hoping you can explain where the money is and how she can access it.'

This was the moment. This was the point when the

expression on her face as she looked at him was pure rage and frustration, just as I had imagined in my powerless days.

'I'll see you in court,' she said, eventually.

'I expect so,' said Edgar, but by the time he had finished speaking she had left the room and gone back upstairs.

I had spent such a long time imagining the moment when I would stand in front of Marina and she would have to recognize I had got the better of her – me, weak, lumpen Ariadne, good for nothing but abuse. It had not been as I imagined it, of course. I was always unimportant in Marina's story. I was an impediment, then a consolation prize, but never, as Ariadne Flood, of any consequence at all. She had wasted no time pondering how she had misjudged me; she had been thinking only of how she could manage the situation to her own advantage.

We heard her footsteps descending the stairs and the front door slamming.

When I went up into the bathroom I found she had scrawled JUST WAIT on the mirror, with lipstick. I was no longer frightened of her, but I changed the locks, just in case. In fact, she vanished, realizing that it was only a matter of time – now I had taken back control of my finances – before she was exposed. Not as a bully, but as a thief. She might have wanted to stay and take revenge,

make my life a misery one last time, but it was not worth
the risk. So she ran away. Once the authorities had the
evidence they needed, though, she proved easy to find.
Running away was not her style and she was not good at
it. She was not, as the prosecuting barrister pointed out
to me, with a suspicion of a sneer, a criminal master-
mind. Though she was, it turned out, a serial offender; I
was not her only victim. Mrs Carmichael had also been
deprived of her assets, her freedom and almost, but not
quite, her sanity, through the loving ministrations of
Marina Blake.

I have a feeling prison will suit Marina. She is tough;
she is a bully; she has none of the feelings that would
make prison hell for most of us – she will miss no one,
she has no sense of shame. I am pleased to think it is so.
Her mother died during her trial, and I am pleased
about that, too. Her life appeared to be a burden to her
but, more importantly, she will not be available as the
only person left to whom Marina can attach herself
when her sentence finishes.

I have been back to hospital for operations to improve
both my vocal cords and my appearance. Mrs Carmichael has moved back in next door and we are the best
of friends. She is helping me with the vocal exercises I
have to do, to help regain my voice. Or, at least, as I
whisper to her, my whisper. She is endlessly patient.

I wave to people passing, now, when I sit in my window, and when I am able, I will go out and speak to

them. Meanwhile, I am as happy as I have ever been, sitting here watching the gulls rising and falling over the waves. I have Bill's books on birds beside me, and am learning to tell one species of bird from another.

EMPTY NEST

I was sitting in a café writing on a sheet of paper when the man at the next table, which was so close to mine I could have jogged his elbow, asked me what I was writing. I looked sideways, keeping my eyes down, and saw that he had a notebook in front of him, and a pen in his hand. This meant he was, maybe, interested in what I was writing and not trying to pick me up. As I had first thought.

'A novel,' I said. 'What about you?'

'Poetry,' he said. 'Tell me about your novel. What is it about?'

I laid my hand over the page in front of me and fingered the edge, as if I was thinking of the best way to describe what I had written. Because I am a very accomplished liar. I am so good a liar that even my husband has no notion that I ever deviate from the truth. I do not wonder whether to lie, any more.

To lie well, though, you have to be within touching distance of the truth.

'It's about a woman who is trapped in an abusive relationship and is looking for a way out.'

The man beside me settled back in his chair. Only the chair was not designed for settling in and especially not for settling back into, as it was a rigid shell of plastic that only accommodated one position – that is, buttocks in the centre, back at right-angle to buttocks. So the end of the pushing-back, settling-in movement left him with his legs straight out under his tea-tray-sized table, impeding the aisle, his arse half over the front edge of the seat and the top of the backrest cutting into the middle of his spine. I noticed all this in the time it took to think 'He settled back,' and wondered whether I should be a novelist after all. I also noticed that he was thin and tall and had a head imperfectly coated with hair. Enough to cover one normal-sized head but divided up to form an inadequate beard and sparse eyebrows with insufficient left over for the scalp. He was definitely not trying to pick me up. He looked like a poet. How pleasing, I thought.

He had begun to say something before I had completed my study of him and I missed the start but understood him to be asking whether I believed the woman in my novel had free will. Was this what I was exploring, in the work? Or the Work, he implied.

'You mean,' I said, 'do I believe her fate was pre-ordained and whatever she does, she is fated to do?'

Apart from never telling the truth, this is my other tactic for making myself impenetrable: when asked a question not readily answered with a lie, or where the appropriate lie is not obvious, seek clarification. It buys time. And it allows you to understand more of what is going on in the mind of the person you are speaking to, while keeping your own thoughts hidden. If the novel idea comes to nothing, perhaps I should write a self-help book. *How to Make Sure No One Understands Who You Really Are.*

'No,' said the poet. 'Not exactly. When I say free will, I mean the absolute ability to act in any way you choose, whatever the circumstances.'

'Why would you not?' I asked.

'The laws of physics would suggest otherwise,' he said, slowly winding in his legs and shifting his bottom to fit himself into the chair in the way its designer intended. The laws of physics depriving him of free will in the matter of how he sat. I was beginning to be interested in this conversation.

'Go on,' I said.

'The laws of physics govern how matter behaves. And we, like all animals, are only matter. Subject to the rules that dictate that, given a certain input, the reaction is predictable and even, using your words, pre-ordained. Whatever we think we have decided to do, of our own free will, is in fact decided for us by how we are pro-grammed to react.'

I thought about this. I took a sip of coffee and a mouthful of cinnamon Danish, shifted my shopping list to one side to make sure the poet didn't sneak a peek at its contents.

'So when a rabbit gets run over crossing the road,' I said, 'you're saying it was always going to cross that road, on that day. That it had no choice but to set off at the moment it did and it was not a possibility it could escape being run over?'

I thought I had phrased this rather well, but he looked unimpressed.

'I'm saying,' he said, 'that if the precise set of circum-stances were to occur at any time in the rabbit's life, it would always cross the road. And by circumstances, I mean its understanding, embedded over the course of its short and dangerous life, of where food and safety lie, and' – he lifted a finger as if to conduct the words he was about to utter to a glorious crescendo – 'its current state of fear and hunger.'

'I'm not writing about free will,' I said. 'Tell me about your poetry.'

I had finished the coffee and the Danish long before he had finished explaining his vision of poetry as the songs all of us have buried within our subconscious from a time before we were born, from before our ancestors were born; songs that only a few have the ability and therefore the responsibility to access and bring up to the surface to unlock the hidden emotions and memories necessary to make us whole. I had stopped listening long before the end of the first poem he read.

I thought about this conversation on Sunday morning as I was cleaning the oven. Specifically, I wondered whether I had had a choice in the matter of cleaning the oven, or not cleaning the oven. Gavin said, at breakfast:

'The oven needs cleaning.' When I didn't answer, he said, 'I suppose I might find time later on today, but I still have some marking I have to finish off when I get back from tennis. How are you fixed?'

Gavin is a teacher and his working week is spent in classrooms and staffrooms and in the conservatory we had built so we could sit, whatever the weather, watching the birds extract peanuts from the bird feeder, seeing the plants in our borders producing leaf and bud and flower and fruit as season followed season, but which turned out to be an ideal space for Gavin to use as an office, and which is therefore out of bounds for idle lounging. I am a dog walker. My working week is spent in the park and along the canal towpath and through the woods on the edge of town. So it is only right that Gavin should be allowed to use his Sunday morning to have fresh air and exercise and I should use mine cleaning the oven.

When did the infinite number of doors that might have been open for me on this Sunday morning start to shut, one after the other, until the options left were reduced to this: clean the oven, or not? Working backwards, I can see that deciding to leave a job I hated in an insurance office to become a dog walker was a choice with implications. Marrying Gavin was another. But the poet had made me think back to when I was still living at home and my mother made me feel guilty for having dusted only the tops of the chairs round the dining-room table, and not the rails underneath. If I believed in free will, the job and the marriage were reversible. I could choose to change. The childhood is done with. Dusted. The matter that is me is forever bound to respond in a way dictated by my mother, so the poet would say.

I decided the oven cleaner had been on the inside of the oven for long enough to make sure there would be a smell evocative of clean ovens next time it was switched on, and wiped it off. I took off my rubber gloves and wrote a note for Gavin – 'Forgotten key ingredient for supper. Back soon' – and set off to visit my mother who lives just a few streets away but much, much further up the high ground of moral smugness that comes with a clean house.

'How good of you to call,' she said, opening the door and looking at my feet rather than my face. I took my shoes off. I didn't need telling.

'Do you have any fresh basil?' I asked. I approach telling lies as I would a sudoku puzzle or a game of chess. Every move has consequences and it is important to consider these in advance.

'Of course.' She led the way to her immaculate garden and into her neat, hexagonal greenhouse where pots of perky herbs held up their aromatic leaves in a mute appeal to be picked, and the geraniums rested in comfort waiting for their moment to blaze in the sun.

There is nowhere to sit down in my mother's kitchen, so we took our cups of tea to the lounge and placed them on the slate coasters with their soft protective underbelly of green felt.

'What have you been doing today?' my mother asked.

'I've been tidying up the spare room,' I said. 'You know how things tend to pile up when you're not looking.' She smiled the sort of smile that, if you are a thin person, you give a fat person who invites you to agree with her that it is a nightmare trying to lose weight. 'You see,' I said, taking a sip of the lapsang souchong, 'I've been wondering about getting pregnant. I was thinking about what we would have to do to the room to make it a nursery.'

My mother looked excited. 'Elspeth,' she said, 'that's wonderful. It would make all the difference.' She picked up her cup in the awkward pause that resulted from her decision not to say to whom or to what it would make a difference.

'But that's just it,' I said. 'That's what worries me. The difference it will make, having a child in the house. How am I ever going to keep on top of everything? Find the time to keep the place clean? Even now,' I laughed, apologetically, 'I find I don't do things like cleaning the oven nearly often enough.'

I had planned this conversation in the expectation that she would tell me, although not quite in these words: 'Fuck the oven, there are more important things in life.' And that this would loosen the grip of my life-long guilt at being imperfect. How naive of me.

'Oh, my dear,' she said, leaning towards me – the chairs were distanced too far from one another to allow for physical contact – 'whatever help you need, I will be here to give it.'

I brooded, on the way home, with my little plastic bag full of fresh basil leaves, on what it is that stops me letting anyone guess that I don't give a fuck about the oven, or the windows, or the skirting boards, or the rails underneath the dining-room chairs.

Sunday nights, after tennis and a supper that has taken a long time to prepare and cook, after the tray for unmarked exercise books is empty, the one for marked exercise books full, we make love. During this part of the weekend ritual I began to wonder whether I should, in fact, choose to have a baby. This is within my control, as I am the one who takes the pills and could therefore decide not to take them. Gavin thinks (and thinks that I think because I haven't disagreed with him) that we should wait a couple of years, but I could choose not to wait. This is the thing about lies: they are stories I have chosen to tell but they hold within them the possibility of truth; they are a different version of life that I could live, rather than pretend to be living.

On Monday, I collected Zora from Angela, Smidge from Belinda and Fluppet from the Andrews family. Before I left, Gavin said:

'I don't want to nag, but do you think you could remember to collect the dry-cleaning today? I was hoping to wear my grey suit tomorrow, for the governors' meeting.'

'I'll try,' I said, and I was still wondering, on the way to Angela's, whether I could face the difficulties inherent in parking near the dry-cleaner's and having to wait, inhaling toxic fumes, for the assistant to match up the little pink ticket I have given her with a blue ticket pinned to one of the hundreds of plastic-covered garments on rails round the room, ignoring me as I point out that it is a suit, not a dress or curtains or an overcoat, that it is a grey suit, in fact I'm pretty sure it is that grey suit, three in from the end opposite the end from which the assistant has started, but the fumes and the tedium combine to prevent the assistant hearing me.

Zora, a miniature cross of some kind, but a nice enough dog despite it, had had a haircut. Angela told me this, as if it wasn't obvious that the hitherto curly-haired bundle was now a razor-cut, diminished version of herself. She was wearing a tartan coat, so well fitting it must have been made for her (I'm still talking about the dog, not Angela).

'Make sure she doesn't get wet,' Angela said. 'I don't want her to catch cold.'

'Don't worry,' I said, 'we're going to the park today and there's not so much as a puddle.'

If we were still covered in hair, as our ancestors were, might we have decided to shave it off and cover ourselves with cloth woven from the hair of a different animal, to prevent ourselves feeling the chill? I doubt it. It would have been so ridiculous it would never have occurred to us.

Zora is a silly name but not as silly as Smidge or Fluppet. None of the dogs is silly, though. They all have the instincts of their kind and will sniff each other's anuses and urine and nose out the leavings of other species to roll in or eat. They vary in their willingness to do or to stop doing what you want them to do or stop doing. They have their own personalities when it comes to amounts of aggression, playfulness; are more or less fearful or bold. If I were able to communicate with dogs in the same way I communicate with humans, I don't think I would lie to them. They wouldn't be judging me, so there would be no point in hiding myself.

I was walking along through the woods in the countryside outside town, when I came across a quad bike parked beside the track, and a man holding a rope which led up to a point in the branches of the tree below which he stood. Beside him was a ladder, leaning upright against the same tree. He was wearing a red hard hat and a yellow hi-vis jacket and he looked at me with a mixture of doubt and hope. Before I reached him, he was making noises that might have been the precursors of speech, or might have been his own thoughts emerging half-formed from his lips.

'Hello,' I said, then, 'Fluppet!' which was obviously, to me and the dog, a command to stop running ahead and come back to me, but this may not have been obvious to the man in the hat because his arm jerked and the rope slipped a foot or two through his fingers.

'What are you doing?' I asked, looking up into the tree. In the absence of leaves – it was March – I could see a large wooden box attached to the end of his rope, some distance up the trunk.

'Putting up an owl box,' he said. I find other people tend not to lie (how do they find the courage?) and the box could, for all I knew, be suitable for an owl, so though it seemed a bizarre occupation, I believed him.

'Why?' I said.

He looked confused, and the confusion, or the continued strain on his arm of holding the rope taut with a substantial chunk of wood on the end, was too much and the rope slipped again. The box slid a little further down the tree. I could see the whole set-up now. The rope went into a little metal eye on the top of the box, then over a fork in the trunk and back down to the man standing beside me wondering how to answer my question. Or possibly trying to work out why, in fact, he was in the position of attempting to haul an owl box up a tree.

'To encourage tawny owls to nest,' he said. His voice lifted at the end of the sentence so he might have been inviting a response, but I didn't have one. 'I don't suppose you could give me a hand, could you? I don't know whether I ought to be asking you, probably not, but I'm buggered otherwise. I was supposed to have a mate to help but he had a domestic emergency, don't ask me what, and I thought, "To hell with it, I can put an owl box up on my own." Only it turns out I can't.'

'Tell me what you want me to do,' I said.

He gave me the rope to hold while he climbed up the ladder and hoisted the box upwards; as he did so, I pulled on the rope and held it in its new, more elevated position while he climbed another rung, and we did it again. The base of the box had to be at least twelve feet off the ground, he told me. I imagined an owl with the sort of eye for angles and distances that snooker players have, knowing at a glance that this box was too low, in relation to the earth, to pass muster as a nesting place. The tree had inconvenient side branches that the box had to be manoeuvred around to make sure it ended up facing away from the prevailing wind. I imagined an owl checking the wind direction and speed like a golfer about to drive off, lifting a wingtip and nodding to itself in satisfaction.

When the box was in the right place, the owl box man fixed it with straps and nails I handed up to him like a nurse in the operating theatre responding to a surgeon, and only when this was complete could I let go of the rope. Which I did reluctantly. Holding it had become important to me in the time the job had taken. Meanwhile, I had learned a lot about owls and the dogs had settled down to watch us working, with the occasional break for a scratch, or a half-hearted attempt to persuade each other to play, having long since finished exploring every smell in the vicinity. The man in the hat and I shared celebratory sips of coffee from his flask.

'What made you take up the job?' I asked. I couldn't work out a route from GCSEs to hoisting birds' nesting sites into branches in a wood.

'It's not a job,' he said. 'I'm a volunteer.' He looked a bit older than me but not old enough to have stopped working for a living, not by two decades at least. He was coiling up his rope, slowly and carefully, not looking at me. Why? I wanted to keep asking. Why are you a volunteer? Why are you not working? It was curious. I am usually happy to invent a story for strangers I meet, and if they insist on telling me about their lives, as they frequently do, without waiting to be asked, I find they are not as interesting as I have made them for my own purposes. They might not have been more satisfied with my version of their past and present than they were with the lives they had lived and were living, but I was. I blame the poet. I sensed I could be standing next to someone, in the woods, dogs at my feet, owl box securely fixed over our heads, who had taken decisions that were not the ones that the pattern in his genetic memory or laid down from his childhood would have nudged him towards.

'I'm writing a novel,' I said, 'about a woman trying to leave an abusive relationship. I'm interested in what makes people go down the paths they choose in life.'

He looked at me as if writing a novel was the weirdest thing he'd ever known anyone do with their time – which was rich, from a man who spent his hoisting nesting boxes into trees.

'It's not so much a matter of choice,' he said, having chewed over what I'd said. 'It's just doing your best to dodge the shit life throws at you. At least, that's my experience.'

'But you did have choices,' I said.

'Oh, yes.' He finished coiling up his rope and began to tackle his ladder, which had ingenious hinges that allowed it to fold up into a neat stack. 'Although I didn't have a choice of whether to be born. Not sure what I would have picked on that one. Not much choice on the jobs on offer. None at all when it came to redundancies. But who I married – I had a choice there, and I got it right.' He smiled, and his face wrinkled up under the peak of the red helmet. He was perhaps older than I had thought at first.

He put the folded ladder, the coiled rope and his tool-box into the trailer behind his quad bike. 'Thanks again,' he said. 'It was probably against the rules to get you involved. You weren't in the risk assessment. So don't go boasting about it on Facebook.'

'Will the tawny owls nest in the box?' I asked.

He shrugged. 'Their choice,' he said, and thundered off through the woods, leaving me with three bored dogs and an empty nest.

I collected the dry-cleaning and hung it up in the hall where Gavin would see it as he walked through the door. Placing it like a note pinned to the wall saying: 'I've been a good girl today'. Not good enough, though. He came into the kitchen holding it in one hand and flicked my earlobe with his other, as he bent to kiss me.

'Legs too tired to climb the stairs?' he asked.

When we were eating supper, he asked where I'd walked the dogs. I made a choice. I told him the truth.

'In the woods.'

'Elspeth.' He put his knife and fork down and reached

across the table to lay one of his hands over one of mine. Mine was still holding a knife. It was a table knife. Blunt. 'You know perfectly well I don't think you should go there. Do you know why?' I nodded. 'Tell me.'

'I might meet a dangerous stranger,' I said. 'I might have an accident and no one would find me.'

'So why did you do it?'

'I didn't,' I said. 'I was teasing. I went to the park.'

He was frowning, now. 'I don't think it's very clever to make me worry about you, is it?' he said. I knew it wasn't. I also knew it wasn't clever to tell him the truth.

I heard on the radio that the team working at the Hadron Collider in CERN have found evidence of a particle that appears to act, or react, contrary to the known laws of physics. They don't understand it but they are excited. I was excited, too, listening to them talking about it. I thought, 'If an invisible, unnameable, apparently insignificant particle can choose to behave in a way that startles the people who thought they knew exactly what it would do in any set of circumstances, so could I.' I set about becoming that particle.

I bought a notebook and a pack of pencils and went back to the café where I'd talked to the poet. I sat at the same table as last time, inches from the vacant space where the poet had sat, with a view of the street. I like this café not because of the poet but because it used to be a bookshop. Once, there were shelves of things to read. I miss its former personality. I felt safe in the book-shop and every book in it – from the Moomin stories to *The Art of War* by Sun Tzu – presented itself as an alter-native to life on the other side of the bookshop doors.

I also like the coffee shop it has become. I feel safe in it, and every other person in it represents an alternative life to the one I am leading on the other side of the café doors; that I don't know what this is doesn't matter. I can imagine it. I am ready, now, to make one of the stories real. To rewrite my life. The beginning is fixed, but the end is still open; it could be anything I want it to be. On paper. And once written, it might look like something a lowly, rogue particle could make happen. It could turn out to be the truth.

HOW CAN YOU
POSSIBLY THINK?

OVERLAP: If two or more activities, subjects, or periods of time overlap, they have some parts that are the same. (*Cambridge Dictionary*)

All the following narratives occurred simultaneously. They can be read in any order.

THE FARMER

Today, a couple walked past. I went outside and watched them. They stopped; she pointed a gloved finger towards the path. He shook his head several times and set off down the track across my fields. I went outside and shouted, as Leanne would have done, though she never will again. These hateful people, trespassing on my land, were bringing back to me the pain of losing her. It should have been Leanne here, shouting.

We were passionate about so many things. Each other, of course. The house, the land, the stock; early mornings when the day held promise and the eggs laid by the hens overnight were sitting on the breakfast table in the oak-wood eggcups carved by my grandfather eighty years ago, and we were the only people sitting in an empty landscape. Evenings passed when our weariness was like a basket of logs brought in to the hearth and laid down with an easeful sense of hard work well done. Leanne was passionate in anger, too, and I was not. She raged against those who did not do as good a job as she believed they should, who did not behave as she thought they ought to. I was indifferent. Why should I let such things bother me, when I was so full of contempt for those people who angered her, leading, as I knew I did, a life more beautiful than theirs? But now, now she is passed. The only passion left to me is hate. How can I not loathe all these blithe and trivial people who behave in ways Leanne would have despised? The sales assistant who laughs when they let your purchase slip on to the floor instead of handing it to you as they are paid to do. The solicitor who explains away his failure to do what he is contracted to do by reference to his own problems – his mother's stroke, the central heating breakdown. The oil tanker driver who lets the hose leak across the yard, creating a slick that he does not understand is his fault. As I face such people, as I deal with them on the phone, I see images of pitchforks, or the axe I use to split the logs. And it exhausts me. It brings back my loss more forcefully each time and I look at each articulated lorry coming towards me whenever I drive to town and imagine what it would be like to turn the wheel just a few inches to the right. But I promised her I would not do that. Treasure the house, she said. Treasure the land.

Leanne always shouted at the people who took one of our farm tracks instead of following the footpath. I never bothered. I felt sorry for them; poor souls who didn't have what I had, who came out once a month, once a year, walked past without understanding the depth and the detail. But she has gone and I was alone with my fury and the thoughtless passers-by were an insult – to the countryside, to the memory of Leanne. So I shouted. I have no idea what words I used. I could hear the echo of Leanne's voice as I spoke, her bold and forceful tone. But my own voice did not sound like that, only irritated, weary. The woman stopped at once and turned to look towards me, then back at her husband, who kept on walking. They had a Labrador, overweight. Both the breed and the condition belonging naturally to the sort of people who come out on a Sunday afternoon believing they have the right to walk where they choose. I went over to where the woman stood. She was holding a map.

'This isn't a right of way,' I said. 'The footpath is over there.'

She flapped the map and looked again towards her husband, called his name. She seemed to be uncomfortable and, had she been alone, I would have smiled at her. I like to think I would have smiled at her, that the rage would not have lasted. Leanne could switch from fury to friendliness in a moment but, being new to rage, I didn't have the control over it that she had. The thought had anyway no time to register because the man began to shout at me and I – how could I help myself? – shouted back. He began to walk towards me. Just as the dog was the sort of dog such people own, so the clothes he was wearing were the sort of clothes such people wear. He was not looking at me as he approached, but kept his eyes on the ground. Despite this, he looked aggressive. The wife said nothing, kept watching the husband, as I was. He stepped closer and all the time my hatred for the man was rising in me like the heat from rotting grass in a compost heap, and all my humanity was being eaten away by it, as the grass is, eaten away and destroyed. I clenched my fists. Leanne would have looked for words to use. I had no words, only rage, and I did not know how to handle that. I wanted this to be over, one way or another. I had no idea what would happen next.

THE HUSBAND

There were so many things to enjoy, and I had been taking the trouble to enjoy every one of them. For a start, I had new boots. We don't spend money until it is necessary to spend money, which is not because it is particularly short, in our household. It is because we have a healthy (I would say) regard for it. Spending money carefully means there is always pleasure in owning something new. I had bought the boots in an outdoor clothing shop where the assistant took the matter of which boots I should buy even more seriously than I did. As a result, I had been more than usually focused on getting this decision right and never mind the cost. It was a treat, to wiggle my feet into those new boots, tighten the laces, take the first few steps. Not just the first few, either; I remembered to be pleased with the sensation of walking in them for a couple of miles, at least.

It was that time of year when the leaves are coming out on the trees, but on not quite all the trees; when the birds are active, squabbling, mating, nest-building; when the wild flowers on the verges are so much brighter and better than my memory of them from the year before. We passed a cluster of trees where there were evergreens and two different sorts of deciduous tree growing together, creating a pattern of dark green and light green, shot through with the brown of a trunk yet to burst into life. I pointed it out to Caroline. 'How lovely,' she said, and I have no idea if she saw what I saw. I am never sure how much Caroline sees – she is quite short-sighted. Sometimes she says: 'Oh, yes, I saw that,' if I tell her that a woodpecker, for instance, has just flown past, but more often she looks where I am pointing and says what she thinks is appropriate.

She is a dreamy one, Caroline. I sometimes wonder how much she would notice or how she would get on in life without me. It is as if, I think, she is caught on a piece of barbed wire and hasn't got the push to free herself, until someone comes along to give her an arm and a tug to get her going again. I see it as my job to give her the arm and the tug, and although I sometimes wish she thought for herself a bit more, made her own decisions, I'd rather have Caroline to live with than someone like my sister Matty, for example, who does exactly what she wants without giving a toss for anyone else. Caroline and I, we look out for each other.

That was the other thing about this walk. Having Caroline there to share the joy of what was all around us. I had given her the map to make sure she didn't just tag along, leaving it to me to decide where we were going next. And I was pleased to be walking with the dog. I know she's too fat and that is mostly my fault because I can't resist giving her the crust from my toast and the fat from the ham in my sandwich, but I don't mind having to stop while she catches us up. Just standing still is an underrated activity, to my mind. Time to notice a gust of wind passing over a field of half-grown corn, or to try to catch sight of the skylark singing itself silly somewhere up in the sky. The dog was part of the pleasure of this walk. Definitely part of it.

But then, the route we were taking became a little dull. The track we were following was difficult to walk on. It was a question of trudging down the ruts in the puddles and mud or making a way along ridges too narrow for comfort. Caroline dropped back; it was impossible to walk two abreast. The dog dropped even further back and there was nothing to see while we waited for her but a field of beans on one side and a bank of hawthorn on the other. And, although I was not yet ready to admit this to Caroline, I could feel my boots beginning to rub, a sensation of discomfort bordering on pain in my left little toe and right heel. It occurred to me for the first time that the attentive assistant might have sold me the most expensive pair of boots he thought it was possible I would buy, rather than the best pair for my feet and the type of walking I planned to do. I was truly reluctant to think this, as the boot-buying and wearing experience had been so enjoyable until then and I didn't want to ruin the memory. So I thought: 'Probably I need to work them in a little. Take them for a couple of two- or three-mile walks before moving up to a six- or seven-miler.'

This was the state of things at the moment we passed an unattractive, isolated farmhouse and spotted a track going off to the left. Though Caroline had the map, I had a pretty clear idea of the shape of the whole walk and it looked to me as if we could cut it short by taking this; the landscape was dull, the dog was a pain, my feet hurt. A shortcut was what I wanted.

'Let's go this way,' I said to Caroline.

'No, we can't,' she said. 'It isn't a footpath.'

It is, if I'm honest, one of the more irritating things about her: her respect for rules. She will follow signs to a car park when there is nothing stopping her parking on the road, just in case parking on the road is not allowed. She studies the rules about recycling as if they were the Bible and follows them as if they were laid down by God. So, at that moment, in view of all the other irritations and despite the previous loveliness of the day, I was cross. So I just walked off down the track anyway, and before long I could hear her wellies – she will never buy a proper pair of boots – thumping along behind me.

We had hardly started down the track when we heard a man shouting. We were in the middle of nowhere. Just the one mildewy old farmhouse, fields of arable. No animals. No fences that would have indicated animals might be hidden by some bush or other, or might be about to be turned out into the fields we were walking through. A track that was grassy, well used, heading straight to a lane less than half a mile away. No gates. No signs. I knew, of course, that the man was shouting because this wasn't supposed to be a track walked on by the likes of Caroline and me. Only by the likes of whatever red-faced farmer or farm labourer had crawled out of his pigsty of a house to object to us doing what was reasonable. I kept walking. Caroline, of course (rules! rules!), didn't.

I turned around to look at him. He was less red-faced, less dilapidated than I'd expected, but more threatening. He was standing over Caroline, who is a small woman, while she fumbled with the map. She seemed to be denying she knew it was not a right of way. She looked to be taking the blame when there should have been no blame. I called out to him that we were just taking a shortcut. He began to shout about private property as if we had committed a crime as bad as, or worse than, touching up his wife or taking his car and driving it away. This stretch of empty acres was his, and however many other acres he had, however rarely he might walk on them himself, he was not going to lend just a narrow strip of them to us for the fifteen minutes it would take us to walk to the other end.

I didn't like the aggression in his voice; I particularly didn't like the way he stood, so close to Caroline, so poised above her like a hawk about to pounce, and the thought that Caroline would be feeling diminished by this awful bully of a man made me furious. I had been going to suggest to her that we continue walking and ignore whatever venomous comments the man might make. He was, after all, powerless to stop us without physical violence, which I assumed was unlikely; I was anyway as tall as he was, and younger. I had been going to suggest this, but instead, I lost my temper. I began walking back towards him, thinking that if he chose to be violent, well, I was more than ready. If that was the only way to end this ridiculous situation, so be it.

Mark stopped walking so I stopped too and the dog, who is overweight, lay down on the grass.

'Straight on or left?' Mark asked. I was holding the map because I don't need reading glasses, so it is easier if I have the map, which also makes me responsible for choosing the path to take.

I had not been thinking of the map, or the path; or Mark or the dog, come to that. I had been following two different strands of thought, letting one go while I pondered the other, then going back to the first.

'Um,' I said, and turned the map until I had a view of the precise area of woods, fields and farms we were crossing. 'Straight on.'

Mark needs reading glasses because he is long-sighted, which means he had a much better idea than I did, in my relatively short-sighted understanding of the topography, of how the brow of a hill to our left related to the field of wheat to our right. He knew where we were in general, while I only knew where we were in particular.

'Are you sure?' he said.

'Yes. Look, there isn't a footpath to the left.'

'There's a track, though. Isn't that marked?'

'Ah, yes.'

'And does it go all the way to the lane this side of that wood?'

'Well, yes, it does.'

'We should take it, then. It's shorter.'

'But it isn't marked as a right of way.'

'Oh, Caroline!' he said, and walked towards the start of the track.

I didn't really care which way we went just as long as I could fall back into the rhythm of walking and return to my two strands of thought, which were these. Firstly, my sister-in-law Matty, who is married to a banker, had phoned to tell me a lifestyle magazine was going to do a spread on the interior of her house. This is the sort of thing that happens to Matty and not to me, and I prefer that it should be so. But as I trudged along at Mark's pace, with frequent pauses for the dog to catch us up, I fell to imagining what it would be like if, for once, this had happened to me. I imagined the type of people who would come to the house to be shown round and take photos; I imagined the interviewer as a younger, prettier version of Matty in vintage clothing and the photographer as a juvenile Benedict Cumberbatch, rueful and shy. I would, I thought, show them every room, as if every room was worth seeing, writing about and photographing. I developed a script I would follow as we went round. The sofa, I would say, had come from the charity shop in town, and the assistant had taken all the cushions off to show us the label confirming it was fire-retardant; otherwise, she said, she couldn't sell it to us. When we got it home, Mark scrutinized the label and decided it could have been sewn on by someone wanting to offload it to a charity shop rather than paying to have it taken away. He lit a match and dropped it on one of the cushions, where it smouldered sullenly, burning a neat hole, then went out. I would show them the hole, but probably wouldn't tell them that Mark has yet to make up his mind whether the experiment proved it was or wasn't flame-retardant. The wardrobe in the spare room came with the house, I would tell them; that is to say, the people we bought the house from failed to take it away, probably because it was too big to go down the stairs. We kept it for the same reason, even though the quantity of clothes it held, if piled neatly on the floor, would occupy less than a third of the space the wardrobe did. In every room, I found, there was a story to tell the proto-Matty and proto-Benedict Cumberbatch in my head. We have quite a few rooms in our house and this little fantasy could keep me amused for as long as it would take to walk the long way back to the car, on the designated footpath.

The interviewer and the photographer, it should be said, were no less fictitious than the diffident but amusing version of myself showing them around.

Secondly, I was thinking about the construction of a liner for the log basket. I had seen log baskets for sale with fabric liners to prevent the debris from the logs dropping through the cracks on to the carpet, and I had found a piece of fabric in my bag of bits I might one day need which would be perfect for the task. Before I started, though, I had to work out the construction: how to attach the sides to the bottom, how to secure the top to the basket. The planning, when everything in contemplation has the chance to turn out perfectly, is often the most pleasurable part of a project such as this, and I was enjoying it.

In the circumstances, I did not want to argue with Mark about which way to go, because such an argument would delay my return to my fantasy and my planning. So I followed him.

We had gone ten yards or so down the marked-but-not-public-right-of-way track when we heard a man calling.

'Excuse me!'

I hesitated. Mark carried on walking.

'Can you stop, please?' said the voice, and I did. At this moment, I knew the day and all my fantasies had escaped from me. I turned round and found an upright, serviceable-looking chap, not young, coming towards me. I looked back to Mark, who was still walking.

'Mark!' I called. 'Mark!' He stopped, every angle in his body expressive of irritation. Slowly, he turned towards me, fixed to the spot, looking at me, not the approaching man.

'What?' he said.

I gestured at the new arrival, who had reached me by this time.

'This isn't a right of way,' he said.

'Oh.' I fumbled with the map as if I had perhaps misunderstood it, or was holding it upside down. 'Isn't it?' I glanced from the map to Mark and it struck me that he was like the patch of green denoting woods, over there, while I was the isolated building, over here, and the tracks connecting us were both linking us together and holding us apart.

The dog, who likes people, other dogs and food as much as she dislikes walking, trotted up and wagged her tail at the stranger. He ignored her.

'It quite clearly isn't,' he said. 'I must ask you to follow the signposted footpath.' He pointed at the regulation green arrow marking the path we had left.

'We're not doing any harm,' shouted Mark, from the distance he had kept between himself and the landowner, for such I assumed he must be. 'It's a shortcut.'

'This is private property!' yelled the man, raising his voice as Mark had raised his, though this was hardly necessary for the purposes of making themselves heard.

I looked from the man beside me on my left, a stranger, to the man a little distance away on my right, my husband, and felt myself to be contemptible in both their eyes. The landowner must think me silly, weak, unable to read a map or take a firm decision on which way to go; Mark would be thinking me silly, weak, unable to stand up to someone who, in his view, was trying to bully us. I could think of no way to recover the illusion that I was not silly. Not weak.

Mark began to walk back towards the stranger. The stranger stood where he was and waited. The dog lay heavily down on my foot and sighed. I began to imagine how this might end, what words might be spoken, actions taken, and I was filled with dread.

WALKING THE DOG

It is an April afternoon on a stretch of farmland no more than five miles from the newest estate on the edge of the old village, but still remote. Reached only by a lane and then a track. The farmhouse is old and squats among its outbuildings, invisible to anyone on the roads and railways of the district. Discoverable only on foot, or by the occupants of any vehicle with a reason for visiting, because no one would choose to drive down the rutted track without a purpose. Anyone standing outside the farmhouse would have a view of fields, hedges, copses, pasture and sky. A landscape that changes with the weather and the seasons. Anyone wishing to watch the world go by should choose a different place to stand.

It is an April afternoon and there is no one standing outside the farmhouse, but there are two people passing by. On foot. A man and a woman, quite young, are walking past the house towards a footpath that leads straight across the fields ahead of them. The man, whose name might be Mark, is slightly plump, above average height, and he is placing his feet down with care. The woman, Caroline, perhaps, is small, slight and walking just behind. They pass the farmhouse and stop where a grassy track leads off from the path, and consult a map. A yellow Labrador, overweight, trudges up to the couple and lies down heavily at their feet. When the consultation ends, the group of three – man, woman, dog – set off at intervals, in that sequence. Mark turns off the path and goes down the grassy track, more briskly, with more determination, although with a just perceptible limp. Caroline waits, watching him, looking round, refolding the map, then she, too, sets off down the track, falling into position behind her husband. The dog, finally, understanding that all other options are now closed to her, struggles to her feet and follows.

Watching them, an observer, if there were one, would have missed a man coming out of the farmhouse. His name, let us say, is Robert. He is unlike the ramshackle house he has just left. He is tidy, apparently strong, without, at first glance, any weaknesses, any cracks or flaws. He looks to be in a place where he belongs, in the context of the house and the landscape. He lifts his head, tenses his shoulders and begins to walk, at a steady, sturdy pace, towards Mark and Caroline, who are retreating away from him down the track they have chosen to take.

'Hey! You!' he calls, his voice cracking, then rising syllable by syllable and ending on a firmer, louder note. 'Can you stop, please?' He sounds peevish now. His voice hints at weakness and uncertainty.

Caroline stops at once and turns towards him. He has almost reached her, and the dog bounds towards him, but receives no encouragement and lies down again. Up to this point, Caroline has been walking with her eyes down, smiling slightly, as if thinking of something quite unrelated to the walk she is taking, but something pleasant nonetheless. Now she raises her eyes to Robert's and she looks stricken, and guilty. She calls to Mark, who stops and turns towards her.

Around this still, upright trio all is as it was before. The light breeze teasing the tips of the newly greening tree branches, the sunlight catching the spiders' webs studded with dewdrops, laced across the hawthorn in the hedge, the chatter of blackbirds in a crab-apple tree, the passing shadow of a kestrel high overhead. It is of no moment to Robert, to Mark, to Caroline, each concentrating on the others as closely as if they were in a room together, negotiating ownership of something precious. Even the dog is keeping her focus on the matter in hand, though she has no idea what that matter is. She stands nearer to Caroline than to Robert but close to both, watching.

Mark begins to move. He is definitely limping. His hair is beginning to thin and his waterproofed, breathable, branded jacket is unzipped and hangs as if zipping it up might be a stretch. He could, as he trudges over the grass, looking down, be a teddy bear. Or a bully. Caroline keeps her eyes fixed on Mark. She is slightly pigeon-toed and is standing with her wellington boots closer together at the toe than at the heel. She is wearing a worn corduroy coat, a scarf and a fairly short, flared skirt that bounced and lifted as she walked. Now she stands perfectly still, as if called upon to model these garments in the window of a charity shop. She might be serene. Or vulnerable.

Robert watches Mark, too. He has his right hand in the pocket of his waxed jacket, playing with whatever is inside, and his left hand clenches and releases in rhythm with the hidden movement of the other. He is frowning. He might be threatening. Or pathetic.

Robert and Mark are both frowning. Mark draws closer to where the older man is standing, finally comes to a halt and looks up. Each man notices that the other is frowning. Mark glances at his wife, then back at Robert, and his hands clench into fists. Robert takes a step towards him, his left hand balled up as Mark's are, knuckles sharp. He pulls his right hand out of the pocket of his jacket, and something comes with it. Something he lets slip from his grasp, if he ever had hold of it. Something small, which drops to the grass at their feet.

They all look down, but the dog is quickest to react, picking up what has fallen. Caroline crouches and pulls it out of her mouth, then stands and holds it out to Robert, who is still frowning, his features rigid. On Caroline's palm is a Fox's Glacier Mint, its wrapper slightly damp.

'I'm so sorry,' she says.

Robert begins to shake his head and, having started, appears to be unable to stop. Without lifting his hands to take the sweet, he lets himself go in a storm of sobs that could almost be the roar of anger that Caroline and Mark believed to be building in him since he first spoke to them. Caroline puts her hand on his sleeve.

'Mate,' says Mark, awkwardly. 'No, mate.'

Robert, still sobbing, drops his chin to his chest and Caroline takes a step closer, puts her arm round his back, being too short to reach higher. Mark takes two steps closer and lays an arm across the other man's shoulders.

Maybe more words are spoken, but if so, they are whispered below the wind and who can say what they are. Then the trio turns and begins to walk back towards the farmhouse, the dog lumbering behind, keeping her eyes fixed on the hand in which Caroline still holds the Fox's Glacier Mint.

It is over now, the incident. The tension leaves them, shoulders relax, fists unclench, heads turn easily one to another. Whatever they each thought was going to happen, it is obvious that none of them anticipated it would end in harmony.

ACKNOWLEDGEMENTS

As always, a professional and dedicated team has been involved in putting this book together, and I am grateful to have all of them on my side, particularly Judith Murray and Jane Lawson, without whom I would still be writing, but only for my own amusement.

I wrote some of these stories for my own amusement, but most of them as part of the submission for a PhD in Creative Writing at Oxford Brookes University. My thanks go to Dr James Hawes and Professor Nicole Pohl, who were the best possible critical friends.

ANNE YOUNGSON is the author of the Costa Best First Novel Award-shortlisted *Meet Me at the Museum* and the acclaimed *Three Women and a Boat*, which was a BBC Radio 2 Book Club pick, and winner of the Paul Torday Memorial Prize for debut authors over sixty. *The Six Who Came to Dinner* is her first collection of short stories, which echo Agatha Christie with their dark edge and sardonic humour as they showcase human foibles and misdemeanours in all their glory. Anne Youngson lives in Oxfordshire and is married, with two children and four grandchildren.